# THE MAZE

# THE MAZE

## MONICA HUGHES

**Harper*Trophy*Canada™**
An imprint of HarperCollins*PublishersLtd*

*To Marie Campbell, with heartfelt thanks for your support and guidance over the years. Bon voyage!*

*Monica*

*The Maze*
© 2002 by Monica Hughes. All rights reserved.

Published by HarperTrophyCanada™,
an imprint of HarperCollins Publishers Ltd

HarperTrophyCanada™ is a trademark of HarperCollins Publishers.

First published in trade paperback by Harper*Trophy*Canada™,
an imprint of HarperCollins Publishers Ltd, 2002.
This mass market paperback edition 2004.

HarperCollins books may be purchased for educational, business, or sales promotional use through our Special Markets Department.

HarperCollinsPublishersLtd
2 Bloor Street East, 20th Floor
Toronto, Ontario, Canada
M4W 1A8

*www.harpercanada.com*

National Library of Canada Cataloguing in Publication

Hughes, Monica, 1925–2003
The maze / Monica Hughes. – Mass market pbk. ed.

ISBN 0-00-639214-8

I. Title.

PS8565.U34M39 2004      jC813'.54      C2003-905647-3

OPM 9 8 7 6 5 4 3 2 1

Printed and bound in the United States
Set in Monotype Plantin

# ONE

## ANDREA

They were waiting for her beyond the school wall, Andrea knew. The knot in her stomach, the shivery feeling down her spine, painted as clear a picture as if she could actually see them through the stones. She'd encountered them her first day at Abbotsville High when they backed her up against her locker, demanding money. The six from Hell. There was Crystal, blonde, with the hardest blue eyes Andrea had ever seen, and Sabrina, obviously trying to be a clone of her tough leader and not quite making it. And there were four others who made up the weight as they pushed her against the locker until she couldn't breathe.

"Come on, insect, shell out," Crystal had hissed between her teeth. "Or else."

"Stay out of their way," one girl advised her on that first bewildering morning. "Holly, Julia, Brenda, Meg—they're of no account. As for Sabrina, she just copies Crystal. And it's Crystal you've got to watch out for, if you know what's good for you," the unknown girl had concluded.

"What's your name?" Andrea had hoped for a friend, but the girl shook her head and vanished into the crowd milling around the lockers. She hardly needed the warning. They looked tough and terrifying, this gang of six, very different from the kids she'd grown up with at her previous school.

Andrea didn't want to find out what "or else" meant. The irony was that she had no money at all, since Father had again forgotten to hand over her promised allowance.

"I haven't a dime, honestly," she'd gasped.

"What about lunch money, insect?" Crystal gave her an extra shove.

"I can pay you in peanut butter sandwiches," Andrea joked, trying to lighten the mood, hoping the Six were not as bad as she'd been warned.

They grabbed her, pinching the soft inner part of her arms till she let out a scream. Crystal's hand was over her mouth before the scream was more than a squeak, and Andrea twisted to get away, kicking in a panic and biting at the hand that threatened to suffocate her.

She was still struggling when a teacher walked by and, like magic, the Six melted away, leaving Andrea rubbing her arms and blinking away tears of pain. The teacher hadn't seemed to notice anything. None of the kids around had offered to help. Nobody said a word to her, not then. But, as she was going into her first class, her arms full of books, another voice spoke in her ear. "You'd better watch out. Crystal's gang is really mean."

"What?" She turned, to see only blank faces. *Not my business*, they seemed to say.

Andrea crouched over her desk, longing to be invisible, but knowing that she stood out like a sore thumb with her long, mousy-brown straight hair, her glasses with lenses like bottle bottoms, and the stupid, stupid, floral skirt that Father had bought for her. "Ladylike," he had said when she protested that *everyone* wore jeans to school. She'd tried to struggle into her old jeans that Mom had bought for her before the family fell apart, but it was hopeless. She had hips now, and that was that. Here she was in the beginning of the twenty-first century, dressed like a girl out of a 1950s sitcom. It was hideous.

At lunchtime the Six grabbed her package of sandwiches and played toss with it until it landed in the garbage can. "Go fetch, insect," Crystal ordered her, and the other five screamed with laughter, ugly laughter that still echoed in her head even after she'd bolted out of the cafeteria.

It didn't get any better in the following days. In her last class a week later the biology teacher accused her of not returning her specimen. *As if I'd want to hang onto a disgusting dissected frog*, she thought angrily. When the frog turned up in the teacher's desk, Ms. Williams refused to believe that she hadn't put it there. Cleaning up the lab as punishment took almost an hour and by the time she got away, the schoolyard was deserted.

This should be good. But suppose the Six hadn't left? Suppose they were waiting to pounce on her, out there beyond the school wall? It wasn't just her imagination. She could feel their presence like a black shadow. "We'll get you, insect," Crystal had whispered as she'd left the science lab. "You'll be sorry."

She shivered. The palms of her hands were wet and she rubbed them against her cotton skirt. She could almost smell her own fear. She was nothing. Nobody here knew her. Off school property anything could happen. She walked reluctantly toward the exit and peered cautiously past the big stone pillar that supported the wrought-iron gate. She knew it! There they were, waiting to get her, all six of them, Crystal in their midst. *Like a swarm of killer bees*, Andrea thought. *With their queen at the heart.* The street was deserted. To get home she'd have to walk right past them. But what if she ran the other way? She might eventually lose her pursuers in the downtown crowds—that is, if she could get downtown before they caught her.

She hesitated by the wall, imagining them beating her up. She licked her dry lips and swallowed hard. Then she took a deep breath, hitched her backpack securely onto her shoulders, and sprinted out of the gate and down the road to her right. She took them by surprise and it was all of five seconds before there was a startled shout and then the unmistakable sound of Crystal's voice. "After her, gang! Don't let her get away!"

She knew enough not to look behind her but to keep running. *Where shall I go? The shopping centre? Closer than downtown.* She might lose them in the crowd there if she was lucky. If not . . . She remembered reading in the local paper of a swarming there only the week before. The security guards had protected the shoppers all right, but by the time the police helicopter landed, it was all over. Five kids ended up in hospital. The swarmers had somehow melted away. Nobody was talking. Nobody had seen anything.

This whole new neighbourhood into which Father had pitched them was fraught with apparent dangers—dangers of which he knew nothing. It was all so different from their old peaceful suburb and comfortable neighbourhood school. *I wish*, she thought . . . but there was no time for wishing. She had to *act. Now.*

*I could take that turn to the river. No, not that way.* She imagined them catching up with her, tripping her. She saw herself struggling in the water, the Six stamping on her hands as she struggled to climb out. No, it was obvious why joggers and dog-walkers stayed away from the river walk once school was out.

There was a stitch in her side and her mouth was dry. *It's not far to downtown*, she encouraged herself.

*If I can just get to the alleys down by the waterfront, maybe I can duck into a shop till they've gone.* Perhaps by then Father might be home and she could phone for help. Help? From Father? Her mouth twisted in a smile. Not likely. But what else was she to do? She ran on, her feet pounding on the sidewalk.

Blindly she turned left, then right. A quick look over her shoulder showed an empty street, but she didn't stop. Her feet seemed to carry her automatically—four, five blocks, and then into one of the picturesque alleys the tourists loved. They were lined with boutiques, each craftily displaying a single dress and no price tags. She could go up twisted wrought-iron stairs to stores selling antique books and stamps, or down moss-covered stone steps into areas behind which were hidden garden shops and places fragrant with homemade soap and candles.

During the tourist season these would be jam-packed with people anxious to unload their cash in exchange for something real, handmade, organic, but now it was September and the alley was almost deserted. There were iron grilles over some of the doors and windows. Andrea began to panic. Maybe the tourist trap was going to trap *her*. Maybe this hadn't been such a good idea after all.

The stitch in her side was almost unbearable. Her legs were shaking and twice she stumbled and nearly fell. *Down the stairs*, an inner voice seemed to tell her. Blindly she obeyed and almost fell down steps slippery with damp into a cool, shadowy, stone-paved area.

She blinked the sweat out of her eyes and looked up. SOFIA'S SHELVES, announced the swinging sign. She tugged frantically at the door and, to her relief, it opened to the jangle of an old-fashioned bell hanging above it. Andrea blundered inside, nearly sending a small table spinning. She pulled the door shut behind her and leaned against it, gulping in air.

*Maybe I'm safe in here*, she thought. *No sign of the Six. But where am I?*

She listened. Nothing stirred. Surely the noise she had made, plus the jangling bell, would bring out the owner from the shadowy depths of the shop. She blinked, trying to adjust her eyes to the dimness, desperately rehearsing what she should say when the owner at last appeared.

A stuffed owl glared at her disapprovingly through its feathery spectacles from atop a bookcase crammed with old leather-bound volumes. More books teetered precariously on a nearby table. A bicycle, surely a museum antique, leaned against a silent grandfather clock that displayed a smiling sun on one side of its face and the phases of the moon on the other. Its two hands pointed upward—to noon or midnight—she could take her pick.

*Someone's going to come out of that back room, asking what I want.* Andrea felt another surge of panic. *What shall I say? That I'm looking for a gift? For Father?*

*Whatever would I give him? For Mom, maybe. Don't I wish I could.* She began to sift curiously through the contents of a deep tray that sat on the counter.

*What amazing junk!* A signet ring with a large and very ugly black stone, a tarnished silver brooch depicting a thistle set with a purple stone, a necklace of carved cameos, cream and brown. Her fingers touched a shiny black oblong object and her fingertips tingled. She drew her hand back in surprise and then picked it up and looked at it more closely.

In contrast with the black enamel finish of the case was an intricate design, a kind of filigree, like a Celtic labyrinth, inlaid on its top. It sat comfortably in her hand, an oblong of perhaps eight by twelve centimetres, and no more than two centimetres thick. What could it be? An old-fashioned cigarette case maybe? She fumbled for the catch and failed to find it. Was it a Celtic design? Or perhaps, more likely, it was a computer circuit, discarded from some broken game.

As Andrea stood in the shadows of this timeless place, she suddenly found her memory flashing back to when she was ten years old, when she discovered, on a shelf in the basement of their old house, a funny old book called *The Story of the Amulet*, one of a series by E. Nesbit. There were fourteen books in all—half of them involving magic—and she had read every one avidly, sharing with no one the excitement this writer's books brought her.

Right now she could feel the same tingle of excitement, the same wonder at the message the writer had left her with: *Magic is real.* "There is a curtain, thin as gossamer, clear as glass, strong as iron, that hangs for ever between the world of magic and the world that seems to us to be real," E. Nesbit had said. "And once people have found one of the little weak spots in that curtain which are marked by magic rings, and amulets, and the like, almost anything may happen."

Back then, when she was just a kid, she took things literally. Now she remembered how she had hunted in antique shops through similar boxes of junk, always hoping that her fingers would land on an amulet like the one the kids in the story had found, an amulet that would open the door to other worlds.

*Five years ago.* Andrea found herself wondering who the E. Nesbit books had originally belonged to. *Father? Not likely. There's certainly no sense of magic in him today, unless whatever weird mathematics he's involved with carries its own kind of magic.* They were more likely Mom's. She remembered that the edges of the pages were fuzzy and worn with rereading.

*Why did I never share with Father and Mom my enthusiasm for these wonderful books?* But five years ago, when she was ten, things were pretty tense. Father was at the university, or in his study, or silent at the dinner table, deep in a book. Cutting her off impatiently if she dared to interrupt his train of thought. Cutting Mom off.

卍

"You can take her if you insist," Father had threatened. "But you'll get a minimum of support money from me if you do! You're the one deserting your family, not I. Think about Andrea instead of yourself. I can promise her a solid education, a future. What have you got to offer?"

Hearing these words again, echoing in her memory, Andrea had a sudden flash of Mom's expression. Beaten. Betrayed. So Mom had walked away without an argument, leaving her with Father.

"Please stay!" Andrea remembered begging, but Mom shook her head sadly.

"I'll try, but I don't think I can. I think I'll die or go crazy if I stay here any longer."

"But what about *me*?"

"Father will take care of you. He'll see that you get a good education. I've got nothing, my pet. I'm useless. He's told me that so often I believe it. All I have to offer you is—nothing."

Mom had promised faithfully to write, but if she had, then the letters must have gone astray, perhaps when Father sold the house and they moved to a condo in a totally different part of town. No longer was there the comfortable school where all her friends were, but the horror of Abbotsville High, where she didn't know a single person, where life was a total disaster and the Six were out to get her.

"I wish we could go back to the way it was before," she whispered, her fingers curling around the black oblong. "I wish a miracle would happen." She held it so tightly that the edges pressed dents into her fingers. But of course nothing happened.

*Stupid*, she told herself. *There's no such thing as magic.*

She stared blankly at the cabinet behind the counter and saw her shadowy reflection staring back at her from a dusty mirror. Tall—she was too tall. Standing out in a crowd was a bad thing. If she were a midget, maybe they wouldn't have noticed her. Hair straight, always falling forward into her eyes. And those awful glasses. No one wore glasses now, but Father said contacts were bad for the eyes, and as for laser surgery to correct her short-sightedness, he'd gone ballistic when she suggested it.

She was still holding the case in her hand, staring absently at the mirror, when a voice spoke from the shadows. "I'm afraid we're fresh out of amulets."

Andrea jumped and the case fell with a clatter back into the box. Behind her a reflection moved, and she turned to see a woman, middle-aged, with thick grey hair falling loosely over her shoulders and down her back. The turquoise and silver jewellery around her neck and in her ears was the same colour as the robe that swirled around her ample body.

She walked past Andrea, her robe sweeping the ground, turned the sign in the window from OPEN to CLOSED, then locked the door. *Click*. Slid a bolt at the top and another at the bottom. *Clunk*.

Andrea had a surge of panic. *Now I'm trapped*, she thought wildly, irrationally. *She must be a friend of the Six.* But before she could move, the woman said calmly, "Now we won't be disturbed. Come through to the back and I'll make tea." As if tea were important when the Six were somewhere out there, circling like hungry wolves.

"I don't know . . . I should . . ."

The woman ignored her stammered protest, turned, and lifted a red curtain that cut off the rear half of the store. Reluctantly at first, Andrea followed her, but as the curtain fell behind her, she felt as if she had been transported to some safe cave at the centre of the world, a place where the Six could not harm her, and where the angry thoughts about her mother and father were stilled.

There was an old-fashioned fireplace, aglow with logs flickering with blue flames from which rose a faint perfume like incense. In front of the fire two high-backed armchairs were drawn up. A copper kettle purred drowsily on the hob. It was almost as if she were expected.

"Sit. Relax. Be calm."

Andrea collapsed into one of the chairs. She felt her spine, suddenly as soft as cotton cord, fold up, and her tense legs went limp. Her clenched hands uncurled. She took a deep breath and felt her eyelids droop.

*No.* She struggled upright. "But who . . . ? Why . . . ?"

"Hush. All in due course. First, the tea."

In a daze, Andrea heard the leaves spilling into the pot, the cushy sound of boiling water poured over them. Her eyes closed and didn't open again until a mug was pressed into her hands. "Here. This will make you feel better."

She opened her eyes to find herself staring into a broad, lined face in which only the eyes were young. These were as clear as a child's and intensely blue; they seemed to look right through her, stripping away all pretences.

"My name is Sofia."

"I'm Andrea . . . Andrea Austin."

She looked shyly away from the penetrating eyes and absorbed the details of the tiny room. It was low-ceilinged, with a high, narrow window that, she guessed, must look out onto the courtyard behind the store, though now the curtains were drawn. The walls were covered with red-and-gold wallpaper, and in front of the fire was a circular rug, the design of which seemed to draw her inward to its centre.

Shelves reaching almost to the ceiling were crowded with pots, jars, and bowls. It was warm, welcoming. Somehow exactly right.

She could almost hear Father's comments in her ear. "How excessive. Emotional. What appalling taste." Just what he had said when she asked for a dreamy wallpaper with ballet dancers and a flowered quilt and curtains for her bedroom in the condo where they moved after Mom left. He ignored her pleas, and her room was painted off-white like the rest of the condo, with polished floors and efficient, dust-free furniture. Sitting in this snug den, Andrea realized that at home she almost always felt chilled and shivery.

She sipped the fragrant tea and waited for Sofia to ask her what she was doing in her shop. What would she say? The idea of a gift for Father was too ridiculous, and anyway she had no money. She needn't have worried. Sofia was holding out the small black case that had attracted her. "You came for this, I believe."

Funnily, she wasn't surprised that this odd woman could read her mind. She smiled regretfully. "It's probably too expensive. Father doesn't give me a regular allowance. I was . . . well, just looking."

Sofia smiled reassuringly. "More than looking, I think. And it's yours. Take it."

As she put the case in her hand, Andrea almost

dropped it. "Why, it's hot—almost too hot to hold. What is it? A hand warmer?"

Sofia shook her head. "Oh, no. Much more than that. But the heat is a sign. It will not respond to everyone. You activated its power when you held it before. That's when I knew that it was intended for you."

"For me? But why? And anyway, I can't afford it. I'm sorry."

"It's not a question of money. You came in here for help, didn't you? Here it is. It's not an amulet, but for you perhaps something more useful. Take it. It will help you find your true self. But remember to go slowly. Think good thoughts and go one step at a time."

"Time!" Andrea suddenly woke up from her peaceful half-trance and put down her mug with a crash. "What am I doing here? I don't have time. Father expects me home. If I'm late he'll be so mad. And they—the Six—will still be waiting for me, if not today, then tomorrow. What I don't have is *time*."

"You have time and enough. You'd be surprised. As for your enemies . . ." She smiled. "You have within yourself the power to overcome them, with the help of this maze." Sofia leaned forward and folded Andrea's fingers over the black case.

Andrea looked down at the case, now no longer hot but comfortably warm. Her eyes followed the intricate silver design that seemed to wind inward to the small stone set at its centre. She felt suddenly disappointed. A maze . . . a kid's toy . . . How could it possibly help her get the better of the Six?

"But how . . . ?"

"It will help you to find your way."

"How can it possibly? It's only a game, isn't it?" *She's just teasing me,* Andrea thought crossly. *Picking up on my dream of an amulet to solve all my problems.*

"Oh, no. It may not be an amulet, but the maze is real." Sofia's voice was sympathetic, picking up her thought so smoothly that it wasn't till later that Andrea realized what an odd conversation it was. "I know it's difficult to understand. I can't help you do that. You must find your own way through the maze. Otherwise it will be my way and not yours. And though I know it's deadly serious—after all, the Six are no joke—it *is* also a game, a game that will help you find your way to the centre."

"What do you mean? What centre?"

"The centre of the maze. And your own centre, of course. That's what it's all about, isn't it? Discovering yourself. Who you really are. Who you want to be."

And at that Sofia pressed her lips together, as if she had already said too much. She got to her feet, shaking out the folds of her robe. "But you're right. It *is* time you were on your way." She lifted the red curtain, ushered Andrea into the shop, and unfastened the door. "Don't be afraid," she said in a matter-of-fact voice. "They're no longer waiting for you."

"How do you know? How can you tell?"

Through the glass she could see the sun still slanting down the slimy steps, as it had when she bolted down them—how long ago? It seemed as if no time had gone by since she pushed open the door. She looked at Sofia, yet another question on her lips. But Sofia only smiled, shook her head, and opened the door for her. As she went out, Andrea looked back. Behind the mysterious woman holding the door for her was the grandfather clock, its hands eternally raised upward, as if time had frozen.

"Th-thank you," she managed to stammer. "C-can I come again?"

"If you have need. You'll get safely home now. Hold tight to the maze. And when you come to use it—" She paused and then concluded emphatically, "Take care. Make sure you have the right intention."

"Sure. Thanks." Andrea wasn't really paying attention, her eyes anxiously scanning the pavement above for a sign of the Six. After all, how could Sofia really know that there was no danger? She slipped the maze into her skirt pocket and climbed up to street level. The alley was deserted. She ran along it to Main Street and caught a bus idling at the stop there. It might have been waiting for her.

Breathlessly Andrea hurried into the apartment, only to find she wasn't late at all. Father was still reading the paper and sipping at the one small glass of Scotch that he measured out meticulously each evening. The glass was still half full. He wouldn't be fussing for his dinner yet. She slipped off her shoes and backpack, hung up her jacket, and hurried into the kitchen.

A salad would be quick, she thought, with yesterday's cold chicken cut into chunks. But summer was over and he'd fuss if there was nothing hot. She ripped open a package of freeze-dried soup, stirred in the water, and washed the lettuce and tomatoes while it cooked. For a while these tasks made her forget the strange meeting with Sofia, and even her fear of her next encounter with the dreaded Six.

"Is dinner ready yet?" Father called from the living room, not actually angry, just impatient.

"On the table in two minutes," she called back, forcing her voice to be upbeat and cheerful so he would not accuse her of sulking. She tossed rolls into the microwave to warm, turned down the soup, grabbed a handful of cutlery, and dashed into the dining room.

*It would be nice if he'd at least set the table*, she thought as she smoothed out place mats, put knives, forks, and spoons exactly as he liked them, the napkins in neat triangles on the left. The chicken salad looked most appetizing in Mom's crystal salad bowl.

She poured out the soup and carried it and the hot rolls into the dining room, just as he appeared in the doorway.

"Only salad? It's not summer any more, Andrea."

"But it's a lovely sunny day, and there *are* soup and hot rolls, Father."

He grunted, sat down, shook out his napkin, and smoothed it carefully over his lap. He lifted his soup spoon, frowned, and put it down again. Andrea took a deep breath.

"The butter. You've forgotten the butter."

"Sorry, Father." She got up too hastily and scraped her chair against the floor. He winced and she bit her lip and took another deep breath as she brought the butter to the table.

"Thank you," he said, his eyes turning to the book beside his plate. They finished the meal without speaking. Usually Andrea dreaded these silent meals, but this evening she was glad for the quiet in which to relive the extraordinary meeting with the mystical Sofia.

After Father left the dining room silently, still immersed in his reading, Andrea cleared the table and automatically put plates and pots in the dishwasher. *Why is Father so cold?* she wondered, trying but failing to remember a time when he'd been more normal. Surely he had been different when he and Mom first met—or why would she have fallen in love and married him? Maybe he had changed with *her* birth. *Maybe it's my fault*, she thought dismally and tried to push the thought away. She thrust her hand into her pocket and felt the black box, no longer warm as if it were alive, but cold and heavy, like a broken promise. Silently she took her backpack to her bedroom, set out her books, tossed the maze onto her bedside table, and began her assignments.

Wrestling over math, with which she had a kind of love/hate relationship, she again almost forgot the events of the day. Carefully she checked the validity of each of her answers. Right. Right. Right. That was the comforting thing about math: You knew where you were—either dead right or out to lunch. Not like social studies, for instance, which seemed very often to be a matter of opinion. Or like real life—or a maze, for that matter—when you had no way of being sure that you were heading in the right direction, making the right choices.

She went out to the kitchen, poured a glass of milk, and grabbed a handful of cookies. She walked quietly back to her room, not disturbing Father, who was still in the living room, absorbed in his reading. Lucky Father, spending his evenings immersed in books, while she had this load of homework. As she munched on the cookies, she caught sight of the black box again, its intricate silver design catching the light. She picked it up, noticing, to her surprise, that it was warm again, as warm as her hand. She cradled it in her palm, admiring the design. What *was* that stone at the centre, cloudy, with little flecks of light in it? An opal? Mother had had an opal brooch, but it wasn't quite like this—not so *alive*. This was beautiful and looked quite valuable. Why *had* Sofia given it to her?

Andrea turned her attention to the design traced on the outside, a silver path winding inward toward the centre. "A maze," Sofia had called it, though to Andrea it seemed more like one of those intricate Celtic designs on classy jewellery. But when she peered at it closely, she began to see that it was indeed a pathway, starting at the outside edge, dividing into two, each path wandering around, dividing yet again.

She sat on the edge of her bed and began slowly to follow the path with her eye. Left or right? She picked right at first since it seemed to lead more directly to the centre. Oops! Dead end. She backtracked and took the left path, intently following its twists and forks. How dark it was getting. She could hardly see anything. She blinked and, without taking her eyes off the maze, fumbled for the bedside light switch.

Her outstretched hand touched a smooth wall where there should be a lamp, a bedside table, a wooden headboard. She shut her eyes tightly, suddenly as nauseated as if she were on a roller coaster or in a high-speed elevator. *Maybe I'm sick*, she thought. *Coming down with a flu bug.* Then the welcome thought: *If I'm sick I won't have to go to school.*

She opened her eyes and her hands flew to her mouth to stifle a scream. Her bedroom and everything in it were gone. She was standing in a shadowy passage, its grey walls vanishing into the distance. She looked up into greyness and down to a smooth grey floor. *I've got to be dreaming. This isn't real. Or maybe it's magic.*

Perhaps magic *was* possible, as E. Nesbit had declared in *The Enchanted Castle*. There was wonder in many of the books she read. In *Skellig*, for instance, the boy finds an angel in a garden shed. And the girl in Michael Bedard's *Stained Glass* belonged in a church window, not in the real world. *Math* was real, but maybe *magic* was real too, as real as math, but with its own set of rules.

"We're fresh out of amulets," Sofia had said when she gave her the box with its intricate silver inlay. *The design looks more like a computer circuit than an amulet. But maybe not a computer circuit, more like a maze through which I must find my way.*

"It will help you find your true self," Sofia had added. "But remember to go slowly. Think good thoughts and go one step at a time."

*What could she have meant? And what's happening now?*

"I traced the design and I guess I was thinking 'maze.' But only as a game. Did something turn it into a real maze? A maze I'm in the middle of right now?" She looked at the smooth grey walls and touched them again.

*Magic? No way! Maybe a computer simulation. An advanced kind of virtual reality game.*

*But how did I get inside it? Not plugged into a computer? No monitor? Well, there's only one way to find out*, she thought, encouraging herself, and began to walk slowly down the featureless grey passage. After a while, the path divided. She stopped. Should she go right or left? Tracing the windings from outside had been easy. Now that she was *inside* the maze, it was very different. The pattern was hidden. There were only grey walls and a grey ceiling. How could she find the centre without a clue or a map? *Suppose I get lost? Suppose I'm trapped in this place that doesn't exist in the real world and I can't get out?*

In this instant of doubt and panic, she heard her name shouted in a voice like thunder. "ANDREA!" Instinctively her hands covered her ears as the voice came again. "ANDREA!" It was Father's voice, loud and distorted, terrifying, at her bedroom door.

She turned and ran back, hoping that the entry to the maze was close by, and somewhat thankful for the excuse to leave. But what would happen if Father were to come in while she was still trapped inside the maze, no longer visible in her room? What would he do?

"I'm coming, I'm coming," she yelled in panic.

"No need to shout." His voice was coldly disapproving, no longer a giant's voice.

"Oh!" Her hands went to her head. The dizziness was back and she staggered and shut her eyes. When she opened them again, she was sitting on the edge of her bed, and Father was indeed knocking at the door.

"It's time you went to bed. Good night, Andrea."

"Good . . . good night, Father," she stammered, hoping that her voice sounded sufficiently normal and not shaky, the way she felt inside. *Take a deep breath, Andrea*, she told herself. "Sleep well, Father," she added.

"Hmm." She heard his slippered feet shuffling down the hall.

After he left, she continued to sit on the bed, staring down at the innocent-looking oblong in her hand.

The wonder of it! The gift of a maze as magical as an amulet or a fabulous phoenix that granted wishes. A maze that would lead her to the heart of some mystery, if she had the courage to follow the path and find her way. *Wow!* The wonder of it blossomed inside her, like a newly flowering garden. *What an adventure!*

The fifteen-year-old Andrea, who could get A-plus in math when she put her mind to it, said out loud, "But there's no such thing as magic. This is the twenty-first century, after all. It's ridiculous."

No, the twenty-first century was far from magical. It was a grim world of dog eat dog, of fighting for your rights or being victimized and swarmed.

"But it happened," she whispered to herself, the ten-year-old still believing in the possibility. "I was there. I can still remember the feeling of the walls, the floor. I couldn't have been dreaming."

"Microchips," her fifteen-year-old self answered briskly. "It's nothing but a neat interactive computer game. Virtual reality. That's all."

She thought about this some more. *If it's only a program why am I scared? And why did Sofia have to warn me? What did she say? "Make sure you have the right intention." What did she mean? Why is the way I feel important in running a virtual reality program?*

She stared at the black case, which lay in her hand, feeling very ordinary, neither warm nor cold. It seemed to have no answers to her questions. Did it have a battery? She turned it over, prying at the edges with her fingernails. It seemed to be a solid, slim rectangle with no access to its inner workings. She gave up and slipped it into a drawer for safe-keeping, hiding it under a pile of T-shirts. Then she felt an odd compulsion to keep it close to her, took it out again, and tucked it into the side pocket of her backpack, securely closing the flap before undressing and getting ready for bed.

It took her a long time to go to sleep. One picture after another flashed before her closed eyes: the Six, pushing her against her locker, pinching her arms; the Six stealing her lunch, hiding her dissected frog in the teacher's desk; the Six looming over her, torturing her. *Don't be afraid*, a calm voice spoke inside her head. And there was Sofia, wise and kind, giving her the maze.

She finally fell asleep and dreamed that someone had given her a precious stone, pressed it into her hand, and then vanished. Who had it been? Whom should she thank? As she worried about this in her dream, she held the stone tightly in her hand, knowing that it was immensely valuable, not because of its worth in dollars, but because of some inner meaning, which she did not yet understand.

# TWO

# ANDREA

Andrea woke next morning with the sense of having grasped something very important—oh, yes!—and was flooded with the most unexpected feeling of happiness, as if her whole body were filled with light. But as she sat up, the dream faded and her happiness with it. It was just another awful day. She had to face Father. And school. And the Six. She felt like lying down again and pulling the blanket over her head.

As Father buttered his toast, freshly made with the whole wheat bread he insisted upon, he broke the accustomed mealtime silence. "I have a most important meeting this evening. Please make sure that you are home directly after school. I need to have dinner early."

*The maze*, Andrea remembered, as the events of yesterday rushed back into her mind, and instead of feeling resentful at Father's orders, she felt suddenly liberated. *He'll be out and I'll have all that time to explore the maze without interruption.* As the thought flashed through her mind, she realized that right now, at least, she was *not* afraid.

"Did you hear me, Andrea? Come straight home after school."

"Yes, Father. Of course." She kept her voice flat, suppressing the excitement that bubbled inside her.

⌘

She was sorting books into her locker when it began again. She felt somebody right behind her and turned, just as Crystal pushed her up against her locker. Crystal's face was close to hers, one hand on her chest, the other around her throat—lightly, but with the threat of worse to come. Lockers slammed. Distant voices chattered . . .

"And then guess what?"

"No way! He didn't!"

"Yeah, I'll never talk to that creep again."

Why did no one pay attention? Come to her help? She tried to cry out and Crystal's hand tightened on her throat. Holly and Julia, Sabrina, Meg, and Brenda huddled around, hiding Crystal's actions from the crowd. *Not that they care*, thought Andrea bitterly. She gritted her teeth and stared back at Crystal, remembering suddenly how, years before, she had outstared a snarling dog. She had been deeply afraid, but she had known instinctively that if she took her eyes off the animal, it would leap at her and she wouldn't stand a chance. She could still remember the way it had growled, deep in its throat, while she stood frozen, her back against a tree, until at last someone came to rescue her.

Crystal's eyes were an intense blue and hard as chips of ice. She had accented them with eyeliner, and there was a lump of mascara on one eyelash. Andrea found herself concentrating on this small imperfection; it somehow offset her feeling of helplessness.

"What do you want?" She pushed back at Crystal. "Excuse me, but I don't like being crowded."

She could see Crystal's pupils contract, so her eyes seemed even bluer. The hand on her throat tightened. "Well, excuse *me*," Crystal echoed. "I need a favour from you, Andy-Pandy."

"Uh-uh!"

"Oh, yes. I need the answers to our math assignment. Like, right now. Okay?" She emphasized each word with a push.

Yesterday Andrea would probably have handed over her answers without a protest. Today was different. She found herself shaking her head. The fingers on her throat tightened and she gagged. The other five huddled close, their arms around each other's shoulders. Someone's foot ground onto her instep. *Holly, I bet*, she thought, seeing the spiteful smile and trying not to flinch. She knew she couldn't take much more. She'd faint or throw up or something. Maybe that'd be the way out—to barf all over them—that'd show them.

In spite of her pain, the thought made her smile,

and she saw Crystal's eyes narrow, a flash of uncertainty cross her face. Then the bell rang. Crystal's fingers relaxed. Andrea pushed her away, spun the padlock on her locker, and hurried down the passage. Math first class, so Crystal and her pals could whistle for a free ride.

But her heart was thudding so hard she thought she'd choke, and she could still feel the pressure of Crystal's fingers on her throat. She swallowed. *I'll have a bruise there tomorrow*. And for a moment she imagined confronting Father with the evidence of their bullying. Maybe he'd take her away from Abbotsville High—let her go back to her old friends in her comfortable old school. More likely he'd make a royal row at school and things would be even worse than they were now—she'd be a *snitch*.

*I'm so stupid*, she thought. *I should have given them the answers. It's just going to get worse the longer I stand up against them.*

*Oh, Mom, I wish you hadn't left. Where are you when I need you?* Gone. Abandoned without even a letter or a telephone call . . . No, Mom was no use. She gulped and swallowed her tears, her hand to her throat. She forced herself to sit calmly at her desk and pay attention to Mr. Canton. She took a deep, steadying breath and found herself remembering the safety of Sofia's small red room, the aromatic tea they had shared. She reminded herself that she did have one friend anyway.

"All right, students. Hand in your assignments."
Mr. Canton's voice broke into her reverie. She
passed up the paper she'd worked so hard on the
night before. *Let Crystal do her own dirty work*, she
thought grimly. Then she tried to concentrate for
the rest of the period against the almost physical tide
of anger she could feel from the Six.

"Andrea!" The sharp voice broke through her
defences. "Calling planet Mars!"

She looked up with a start as a giggle rippled
through the class. "Sorry, Mr. Canton."

"An excellent paper. You really seem to have
grasped the underlying principles. You're not just
working out the problems by rote. I want to talk to
you after class. As for the rest of you, I despair. We'll
go over matrix theory again tomorrow. This is basic,
students. If you want to survive the accelerated math
program in grades eleven and twelve, you'd better
come to terms with the basics right now."

Andrea slumped down in her desk, wishing once
again that she was invisible. *Maybe it'd be simpler just
to act stupid*, she thought miserably, feeling the tide
of resentment, not just from the Six, but from the
whole class. *Teacher's pet.*

"So, class, tonight you'll read the chapter over-
view and *try* to answer questions six through twelve
correctly." His voice overrode the groan that ran
around the room. "Like I said, if you want to suc-
ceed in engineering or computer technology, it all

begins here. Now, off you go. Andrea—a word."

She stood by his desk, wondering what was coming. So far, nothing good had come her way from Abbotsville High, but Mr. Canton's face was friendly as he looked up at her. "Your work is excellent. I'm wondering what you would think about enrolling in an enrichment program in your spare time?"

Andrea groaned inwardly. Spare time? After class and assignments, cleaning the house, marketing, cooking—what spare time did she have? He must have seen the expression on her face. "Come now. It just means giving up a half hour of TV a night, that's all."

"But I don't watch TV. Father doesn't approve. And anyway, there really isn't any time, Mr. Canton. I'm sorry. I'd love to . . ."

"Okay. Don't distress yourself. But I don't want you getting bored and turned off math. That would be a shame. I think you'll be more stimulated if you do the advanced questions at the end of each chapter from now on."

"As well as . . . ?" Her heart sank.

"You really don't have much time? You're not just making excuses, are you?" He frowned and then, looking at her expression, seemed to relent. "Try a few of the advanced questions and see how it goes. Of course I won't penalize you if you can't manage it. All right. Off you go."

As Andrea hurried to her next class, she suddenly realized that she now had the perfect reason not to hand over her finished assignments to the Six—or, of course, she could hand over the answers to the more advanced questions and let Mr. Canton find out for himself that the Six were stealing them instead of doing their own work. This cheered her up enough to get through the rest of the morning's work without any more worries.

Lunchtime. At least she lunch money from Father today. She filled a tray and looked anxiously around. That table in the corner would do. There was room for one more on the end, and there was safety in numbers—maybe. As she turned, someone bumped into her, jolting her tray so that the tomato juice spilled and flooded everything.

"Oops, sorry about that!" It was Holly, a big smile on her face.

"Give me that and start over." The woman server had seen what happened and took the tray from her. "And you, kid, watch it!" She frowned at Holly.

By the time Andrea got a fresh tray and collected her lunch, the empty place she had hoped for was filled. She had to settle for the end of a table with several free spaces left. As she put down her tray, the students looked at her and at each other, and there was an awkward silence. She could almost read their minds. *Trouble!* And they wanted no part of it. She couldn't really blame them, but she wanted to shout out, "Lookit, you guys, it could be any of you. You'd want to have friends then, wouldn't you? People who'd stand up for you." Instead she gave a weak smile, sat down, and began to eat.

She had barely swallowed her first mouthful when the Six appeared behind her. "Move over, you lot," Crystal ordered and despairingly Andrea saw the others meekly shuffle out of the way.

Holly slammed her tray down on Andrea's right, and Sabrina pushed in on her left, just as Andrea was lifting a mouthful of salad. It went flying. "Oops. Did I shove you? Sorry about that."

The other four sat around her. She tried to ignore them and began to eat as quickly as she could so she could get out of there.

"Pass the salt, Sabrina." Crystal leaned across in front of her, her arm outstretched. "Gee, this lid's kind of loose." She fiddled with it and the top spun across the table. Crystal upended the shaker over Andrea's plate.

"Careless me! Now look what's happened. Never mind, Andy-Pandy. Salt's supposed to be good for the brain, isn't it?"

The other five roared with laughter. Andrea pushed back her chair. Her hands were shaking and she blinked back tears. She picked up her tray and tried to make a dignified exit, her head high. The food monitor tutted at the unfinished food. "You girls are so wasteful. Don't take it if you're not going to eat it! You know the rules. I'll have to give you a penalty for that. Name?"

"But it's inedible!"

"Any complaints about the quality of the food can be directed to the cafeteria board. Name?"

"Andrea Austin." Andrea tipped her meal into the garbage, dropped her tray on the rack, and stormed out.

By mid-afternoon she was starving and would gladly have swopped the mysterious maze for a chocolate bar. *Home early*, she reminded herself. Father's got that meeting. She planned what she would cook. Grilled sausages would be quick. And rice. But Father'd want something green. Maybe a salad. She'd have to pick that up on the way home.

Her stomach gave a huge, thunderous rumble at the thought of food and she pressed her fist into her tummy and tried to ignore the giggles around her. Ms. Brookes looked up vaguely, as if acknowledging the "noises off," and then went on reading from the witches' opening scene in *Macbeth*. "When shall we three meet again in thunder, lightning or in rain?" Andrea's stomach rumbled once more and the giggles became laughter.

"Who *is* making that noise?"

"Sorry, Ms. Brookes. I can't help it."

"Go get a drink of water and *try* not to disrupt the class, Andrea."

As soon as class was over, Andrea collected the books from her locker, stuffed everything into her backpack, and ran for the exit, making sure she was ahead of the Six today. Except she had to stop at the corner store for salad greens. There was a line-up at the counter and the owner seemed to take forever making change. The shortcut across the park would save time, she decided, looking anxiously at her watch and tucking the lettuce into her backpack.

As Andrea crossed the road to the park entrance, she had second thoughts. *Maybe going through the park isn't such a smart move. The street would be a lot safer.* But a glance at her watch told her she was already running late. She made up her mind and started jogging briskly along the main path that ran diagonally across the park.

It wasn't deserted. There was a woman walking two Samoyeds. Another with a pram. A jogger brushed past her and she jumped, her heart pounding, but it was only a man in his fifties, who muttered an apology and puffed on. A mutt of a dog chased a ball in the distance. *There are loads of people around,* she told herself. *I'm perfectly safe here. I can't let those guys ruin my life.* Sweat trickled down her face and she wiped it away. She longed, for the millionth time, to be back in her comfortable old school with the kids she'd known since kindergarten, where hazing and swarming were unknown.

The path narrowed just ahead of her, two beds of rhododendrons crowding on either side. No longer in flower, they looked dark and menacing, but once past them she'd be almost across the park. *Boil water for rice*, she told herself to take her mind off the spookiness of the bushes. *Wash the lettuce and make dressing. Too bad Father won't let me buy bottled dressing.* She'd tried cheating by buying ready-made stuff to save time, but he'd looked through the fridge and thrown it all out, *and* given her a lecture on chemical additives. These thoughts tumbled through her head as she hurried across the park, almost running.

As she passed the last of the rhodos—*almost home free*, she thought with relief—they burst out from behind the bushes. It happened so quickly that she didn't have a chance to escape. She managed to slip off her backpack and use it as a weapon, swinging it in front of her from left to right. She caught Brenda on the first swing and Meg on the second, but they weren't the real enemies anyway. She wasn't afraid of *them*.

Someone grabbed her from behind, hands cruelly pinching her midriff, and yelled "Get that pack!" It had to be Crystal or Julia, because Holly and Sabrina were in front of her, tugging at her backpack. She hung on and found herself being dragged forward. Someone's foot shot out between her legs and she stumbled and fell heavily onto the gravel path, grazing her hands and knees. She grunted as the breath was jolted out of her. A foot stamped on first one hand and then the other, and her backpack was snatched away. She struggled to catch her breath and yell for help. Nobody seemed to notice what was going on. Nobody ran to her rescue or shouted at the Six to stop. She tried to get to her knees.

"Sit on her, you useless lumps," Crystal ordered Meg and Brenda, and Andrea grunted again as their weight landed on her back. "What's this?" She tossed the plastic grocery bag to Sabrina.

"Just lettuce. My, what a nerd!"

"Give it here," Holly yelled. "We'll make a salad." She and Julia began to shred the lettuce and scatter the pieces over Andrea's prone body.

"Too bad we don't have any dressing!" Julia screeched with laughter. "We could have a tossed salad. What else is in her pack?"

Crystal upended it and Andrea saw her books and binder fall in the dirt. "Hey, this binder's really loose." Crystal pulled on the snap and let the pages scatter in the wind.

"Please don't!" Andrea wailed.

"Oh, not to worry. I'm sure you can redo all this. You're *so* clever."

"Look, this'll do for salad dressing. Sunscreen? In September? What a nerd!" Sabrina tossed the bottle to Holly.

"Just the thing. Out of the way, you two, unless you want to get splashed. Here we go."

Andrea could hear the cream glugging out of the bottle and splashing over her back and legs, running clammily down her neck, soggy in her hair, smearing her glasses so she could hardly see. Some of it ran into her mouth and she spat it out. She tried again to struggle to her feet, but their grip on her was too strong.

"Now, we should just toss her in this. Take her legs, Holly. One, two—"

"Wait a minute. What's this?" Sabrina held up the black maze. Andrea opened her mouth to scream *Let it alone!* and then shut it again. *It's not really a magic amulet*, she told herself. *Just some kind of interactive game. Not worth sweating over.* But it was. She was sure it was.

"Give it here." Crystal snatched it from Sabrina's hand. "What's inside? Where's the catch?" She fumbled, gave up, and dropped it on the ground. "Stupid thing!" She stamped on it.

"Let me look. I bet I can open it." Sabrina reached out for it, grabbing Crystal's foot.

It happened so quickly that afterwards Andrea was never quite sure exactly *what* happened. There was a blinding light, a prickling surge of energy, and a smell like a shorted circuit or lightning. But out of a clear sky? Her eyes automatically shut at the flash. When she opened them again, the girls' weight on her back was gone. She could hear them screaming. They weren't paying any attention to her. She struggled to her knees, wiping the sunscreen from her face, pushing back her slimy hair.

"Where've they gone?" she heard Brenda scream hysterically.

"Into the bushes, of course. Stop that caterwauling and go look." That was Holly's voice, bossy, but with a quaver in it, like she too was scared, thought Andrea. She scrambled to her feet and began stuffing her belongings back into the backpack, chasing after the occasional fly-away looseleaf sheet. She scooped up the maze, lying apparently undamaged on the path, and tucked it quickly in among her notes. *What did Brenda mean, "Where've they gone?"*

Thankful to escape and not looking back to see what had happened, she began to run as fast as she could to the exit, gasping, tears running down her face. Two middle-aged walkers with a dog stopped and stared. A runner veered quickly out of her way. Had they seen the swarming? Did they care? Then she realized that it was *she* they were avoiding, that she was plastered all over with torn lettuce stuck on with the creamy sunscreen. *I must look quite crazy.* She tried to pluck off pieces of lettuce as she ran, and wiped her face with her spare hand, smearing tears and lotion. She dared not stop to clean her glasses, but peered through the smeary lenses as she approached the busy intersection beyond the park. A driver hooted angrily and she leapt for the curb, her heart pounding. A flash of light. A power surge. From *where?* And the girls screaming . . .

The security man outside their condo laughed as she ran up. "Very tasty. Is that French dressing or Thousand Islands?"

"Very funny." She pushed past him and took the elevator to the eleventh floor. Father was standing in the hall, waiting for her. "I told you to be home early. Weren't you listening? And what on earth is that on your clothes? In your hair?"

Andrea gave a humourless laugh. "Your salad, Father. Sorry about that." She dumped her backpack in the hall and pushed past him into the bathroom. She tore off her clothes, shedding greasy lettuce leaves on the floor. She had the quickest shower and shampoo in history, wrapped her hair in a towel, anointed her grazed knees and elbows with ointment, washed her glasses—luckily they hadn't been broken—and shot into her bedroom. Found a housecoat and slipped it on.

With her hair still wet, she skidded through to the kitchen, measured out rice and water, turned on the grill, and defrosted a package of spinach. She whirled into the dining room, noticing with faint despair, but without surprise, that he'd made no attempt even to set the table.

A total calm efficiency, fired by adrenalin, had taken over, and she went along with it on automatic pilot. Even when Father called to exclaim about the mess in the bathroom, she didn't lose her cool. "I can get your dinner, Father, or I can clean the bathroom. Short of finding a way to clone me, I can't do both at the same time."

"No need to be impertinent."

"I'm not," she muttered, as she stooped to turn the sausages under the grill. Too bad Father wouldn't countenance TV dinners. She could have zapped them in the microwave and they would be eating right now.

He paced between kitchen and dining room, looking at his watch. She took a deep breath. "Maybe you could phone and tell them you'll be a few minutes late."

He sighed heavily. "I can't believe this! What on earth were you doing?"

"Being swarmed," she snapped. "Do you know what that means, Father? It doesn't mean being attacked by bees—not even killer bees. But the results can be as horrendous."

"I know what it means. But how could you allow yourself to get into such a situation? Surely . . . ?" He blinked and took off his glasses to stare at her. "If you had come straight home as I asked you—"

"They jumped me, Father. Six of them to one of me. I wish you could understand. I'm the new kid in school. Everything is wrong with me—my clothes, my hair, my glasses." Andrea gulped down angry tears. Father was staring at her in bewilderment. *He really doesn't understand.* "You see, I'm brighter than most of them, but I've been too stupid to hide it. That's my mistake, Father. I confess. I should have dumbed out and settled for B's on my assignments.

B's are safe, which is ironic, since it wasn't the bees but the A's that made them swarm." She could hear her own voice rattling out of control. She took a deep breath.

"You're telling me your fellow students did this to you? But . . . your school has an excellent reputation. I was most careful . . ." He shook his head.

"Sure, for academic achievement maybe. Rah-rah! But it hasn't helped that I stand out like a sore thumb with my dumb skirts and glasses and no makeup. And don't tell me the teachers'll stop it. They just turn a blind eye to what's really going on."

She pulled out the broiler pan, served up sausages, dumped rice and spinach into bowls, and carried the lot through to the dining room.

"If you'll excuse me, Father, I'll eat later. I've got a bathroom to clean out."

She whirled out of the room, leaving him with his mouth open. It wasn't until she finished cleaning up the bathroom that she realized that she had actually stood up to Father and that, moreover, the sky hadn't fallen in. The front door slammed and she was alone. Free to explore the mysterious maze? Not till she'd eaten, cleaned up the dishes, done the laundry, and sorted out the mess the Six had made of her notes.

Andrea pushed the weird incident out of her head. *Nothing to do with me*, she told herself. *Just the Six playing stupid games*. She was still trying to make sense of the notes scattered during the swarming when the doorbell rang. She looked at her watch and frowned. Nine-thirty. By the time she'd cleaned up, eaten her warmed-over supper, and stacked the dishes in dishwasher, the evening was half over. And she *still* had assignments to finish. Had Father forgotten his key? She sighed impatiently and went into the hall. "Yes?" she said into the intercom.

"Andrea Austin?" A strange male voice.

She frowned. How did the man get past security downstairs? "Who wants to know?"

"City police."

Her heart pounded. Had there been an accident? Father? She slipped the security chain onto the door, unlocked it, and opened it a crack. There were two men in uniform. "May I see your ID, please?"

They held up cards, which looked genuine enough, as far as she could tell. The faces seemed to match the photographs. "Wait a minute." She closed the door, slid off the security chain, and opened the door. "Is something the matter? My father? Has there been an accident?"

"Nothing like that. May we come in, Miss Austin?"

"Sorry." She blushed and stood aside to let them into the hall.

"I'm Detective-Sergeant Ted Miles and this is Constable Brian Fraser."

"How do you do?" Andrea said formally, while her brain skittered. *What can they want? Brian has a nice smile and kind eyes, but that Ted—I can tell he doesn't trust me. Narrow eyes and a tight mouth. I feel guilty just having him stare at me. But guilty of what? What am I supposed to have done?*

"We're inquiring into the whereabouts of two of your friends, Crystal Newton and Sabrina Collins."

"Whereabouts?" Andrea looked at them blankly. "And they're certainly not *friends*. Oh, did somebody report the swarming? Is that what it's about?" She felt a sudden sense of relief. Those people in the park. The woman with the baby carriage. The ones walking dogs. They weren't totally insensitive after all. Someone had cared enough to report . . .

"A swarming?" Detective Miles frowned. "Someone was swarmed?"

"Why, yes. Me. You mean nobody reported it? Then what are you doing here?"

"Perhaps we could sit down and you can tell us exactly what happened."

"Yes, of course. I'm sorry. It's just, well, we've never had the police around here before." She led the way into the living room, they sat down, and she explained what had happened on her way home from school. "Then for some reason, they suddenly let me go," she concluded. "So I grabbed my stuff and got out of there. I'm *still* trying to sort out my notes."

"Was that the first time you were hassled by this group?"

Andrea hesitated.

"The truth, please."

"It's just that I know they'll be far worse if I complain. I didn't mean to . . . I mean, I thought you knew all about the swarming and that's why you're here."

"So you have been hassled before?"

"Since school started." Andrea shrugged, trying to pretend that it wasn't really a problem. "I knew moving to a new area—to a high school where I didn't know any of the kids—I knew it wouldn't be easy. I just didn't know it would be *this* hard." She twisted her fingers together, looking down so he wouldn't see how close she was to tears.

Detective Miles sighed. "If people would only . . ." He broke off. "But, heck, I can remember what it was like at your age. No snitching. But that just gives more power to the tough guys. You know that, don't you?"

Andrea cleared her throat. "Sure." Then she looked up, a puzzled frown on her face. "But if you didn't come about the swarming, why are you here?"

In the silence that followed her question, she was uncomfortably aware of the intensity of his gaze. His eyes were a very pale blue, so that the pupils showed up extra dark, like twin-barrelled guns aiming directly at her. She told herself not to be fanciful and forced herself to turn away from him, to look at the other policeman, Brian Fraser, who seemed to have the friendlier face. But now *his* eyes were on his notebook, which rested on his crossed knee, and his pen was in his hand, ready to write down whatever she said. That was almost as scary as the other man's eyes. The silence was unbearable.

"You were asking me about Crystal and Sabrina. What's happened to them?"

"Ah! Do you know that something has?"

She shook her head. *They're playing with me, teasing me,* she thought. "I don't know anything. I left them in the park. But you're here, asking about them, so what's happened?"

"They're missing."

"Crystal? Sabrina? How? When?"

"From the park. From the time when you were all together, Miss Austin. Only there wasn't any mention of swarming. Just that there were six of them—and you. According to two of the girls—Meg and Brenda—Crystal and Sabrina vanished into thin air." He cleared his throat. "Obviously that's not what happened. The girls were a bit hysterical at that point. But what *is* clear is that they have gone. Apparently the others searched the nearby bushes and when they got back to the path, you had vanished too."

"I didn't *vanish*! That's ridiculous—crazy. When they got off me, I picked up my stuff and ran home. I was late. I had to get Father's dinner. I couldn't figure out why they'd suddenly left me alone, but I was just thankful to get away."

"And that's all you know? You haven't seen Crystal or Sabrina since? They haven't phoned?"

Andrea shook her head. "I don't understand. Where could they have gone?" Her words sounded forced and artificial to her. *A light. A power surge. I can't tell them about that. It's crazy. As crazy as if I said they'd been abducted by aliens*. She stared silently at the two, willing them to go away.

The detectives got to their feet. "I expect there's some logical explanation," Ted Miles said smoothly. "We'll be talking to you again later, of course."

"But I don't know anything—"

"You were at the scene. Frankly, your version of events doesn't exactly match with the testimony of the other four young ladies . . ." His sentence trailed off and he drilled her once again with those pale eyes.

She flushed. "I *am* telling you the truth."

Neither of them spoke, only nodded to her as she saw them out and closed the door. Ten o'clock already and she still had her assignments to finish. Her notes were in order, though crumpled, and there was a muddy footmark on one of her books. She shook her backpack and the black maze game slithered out. She stared at it and reached out to touch it cautiously. It had been almost red hot when she tossed it into her pack, she remembered, as if it had been subjected to an overload of energy.

Had she imagined the brilliant light, the surge of energy, the smell like an electrical short-circuit? What could that have to do with the girls' disappearance anyway? And the maze? What was its connection to what had happened? *It's only a game*, she told herself. *A virtual reality gizmo*. She touched it again. Smooth enamel. Just a small black box with a tracery of silver on its top, a bit like a computer circuit. It wasn't hot now. Maybe she'd imagined that. She tucked it away among the T-shirts in her drawer— out of sight, out of mind. But where *had* Crystal and Sabrina gone?

She turned to her social studies notes and tried to concentrate. People didn't just vanish into thin air, did they? The words blurred in front of her. Some time later Father came home and knocked on her door. "Time your light was out."

"Yes, Father. Good night." She put away her stuff. *Tomorrow* they'll be back in school. Everything'll be normal, she told herself firmly as she got ready for bed. Then she thought: normal? *Normal is having the Six on my back! Why in the world would I want that?*

# THREE

## ANDREA

At school on Wednesday morning the mood was electric, flickering from locker to locker. Andrea caught snatches of whispered conversation as she pushed through the crowd. Was it fear? Anything seemed possible. She listened, her heart suddenly pounding, remembering last night's police interrogation.

". . . haven't found the bodies yet."

". . . pervert."

". . . maybe a serial killer."

". . . Remember those unsolved murders last year? Well . . ."

Could they possibly be talking about Crystal and Sabrina? She swallowed a sudden rush of panic. She sorted her books and set off for her first class, telling herself that they must be talking about something totally different, something that had been on the morning TV newscast, something she would have missed, since Father refused to have television in the house. She saw Julia, Meg, Holly, and Brenda, and her eyes scanned the room for Crystal and Sabrina.

They *were* missing, just as the police had said. *Weird*.

She became suddenly aware that everyone in class was staring at her, staring and then looking away quickly. It was very unnerving. Her stomach gave an uneasy lurch. What was going on? What exactly had the four told them?

"What is it? What's the matter?" she whispered to the girl in front of her.

Marilyn turned and stared at her, her face a mixture of fear and curiosity.

"You're kidding me? You mean you don't *know*?"

Before she had a chance to answer, the principal, Ms. Anderson, strode into the classroom and up to the front. "Attention, students. The police have been in touch with me. I will shortly be addressing the whole school on the intercom, but since it affects everyone in your grade more immediately, I intend to talk to you first. As you have no doubt heard, Crystal Newton and Sabrina Collins are missing and have been missing since shortly after school yesterday afternoon. There is *no* suggestion of kidnapping. No demand for ransom has been received. Nor is there any reason to suspect that a murderer is on the rampage in Abbotsville, nor is there any truth in any of the other outlandish rumours I have already heard this morning. The girls are missing and *that is all we know*. I presume they have run away. Since both Crystal and Sabrina are in this grade, I am appealing to you now. Did they talk to anyone here about some plan to take off? Even a casual word. If anyone has any information that can shed light on their disappearance, please speak up now."

She looked around the classroom. Andrea could feel her cheeks grow hot and her palms sweaty. She clenched them in her lap. "Very well," Ms. Anderson continued. "The city police intend to interview every person in the school, if necessary, beginning with your grade. Be truthful and please keep your imaginations under control! The counsellor's office is being made available as an interview room. You will be called alphabetically. Once you have been questioned, go straight to the library. Take your English assignments with you and work quietly until all the interviews have been completed. Do *not* discuss your interview with your fellow students. Is that clear?"

"Why do you suppose we're banished to the library?" someone whispered.

"So we won't have a chance to compare our stories, dummy," someone else snapped back.

Andrea saw the four glance at each other. They, at least, would have had all last evening to get *their* stories together. Would anyone believe *her* version of events?

She jumped as her name was called. It was a pain having a name that began with A: double-A, in fact. But surely they would have no more questions after last night? This interview would be just a formality.

She clutched her Shakespeare to her chest as if it were a lifesaver and scurried to the door.

She was only too familiar with the counsellor's office; she had been here before, in her first miserable week, as Ms. Kent had tried, with infinite tact, to get Andrea to talk about her family, her feelings, and her general attitude to Abbotsville High. It had been an awkward and embarrassing experience and, as she approached the room again, the same sense of being helpless and tongue-tied overwhelmed her. She scuttled in, already feeling guilty, though she had done nothing wrong that she knew of.

Behind the desk today was another woman, a short, neat brunette, not much different from the school counsellor, and, by the window, a uniformed constable, notebook in hand. Andrea swallowed, took the chair drawn up in front of the desk and laid her Shakespeare on her knees, clutching it with her fingertips, hoping no one would notice her trembling.

"You're Andrea Austin? Hello. I'm Detective Rooke. Just a few questions. Nothing to be afraid of." Her voice was pleasant, her appearance unalarming. No different from Ms. Kent, but, like Ms. Kent, loaded with personal questions she would be forced to answer.

"But I told the two officers everything I knew last night."

"Of course you did. We're just going through the whole class, trying to get a profile on the missing girls. Some clue as to where they might have gone. Do you understand?"

Andrea nodded dumbly.

"Good. You know them both—Crystal and Sabrina?"

"Yes."

"Are they special friends of yours?"

"Goodness, no!" The denial came out more strongly than she'd expected.

"But you were together with them in the park after school yesterday, weren't you?"

"That doesn't make us friends." Andrea took a deep breath. "Look, I told the other officers about it. I was going across the park on my own and they swarmed me—the six of them."

"Six?"

"Crystal and Sabrina were the leaders. Then Holly and Julia—they were pretty mean too. And Meg and Brenda—sort of hangers-on. I wasn't afraid of *them*."

"And was yesterday the first time these six students had ganged up on you?"

"No. They've been on my case since the first day of school. It's just been getting worse. I was able to get away from them two days ago, but yesterday they caught me crossing the park."

"What did they actually do?"

"Grabbed me, tripped me, and sat on me. Twisted my arms and stamped on my hands."

"Not a dangerous swarm then?"

Andrea looked up, shocked. "I thought it was. They'd threatened me earlier. Crystal and Sabrina freaked me out. I really felt they were capable of anything."

"But in fact nothing much happened, did it?"

Andrea shrugged. "Depends how you look at it, I guess. They tripped me and then sat on me so I couldn't get away. Then they messed up my assignments. They tore up the lettuce I'd bought for Father's dinner, scattered it over me, and then poured sunscreen on . . ." She stopped, frowning. "I expect you think that's pretty funny, eh?"

"No, I think it was kind of mean, but not exactly life-threatening. What happened next?"

"One of them yelled. I'm not sure which of them. Then Meg and Brenda jumped off my back and Brenda shouted, 'Where've they gone?'" She frowned, searching her memory. "Someone—I think it was Holly—ordered the others to search the rhodo bushes."

"Is that where they'd gone?"

Andrea shook her head. "I've no idea. I couldn't see and I didn't hang around to ask. I just got up, grabbed my stuff, and ran."

"And that's it? Nothing more?"

Andrea shook her head. What else could she tell them? *Bright light? Energy? Like they'd been sucked into another dimension?* They'd think she was nuts.

"Neither of them phoned you last night?"

"No. I already told—"

"Bear with me, please. So you ran home. What did you do then?"

"Cleaned up. Had a shower. Got Father his dinner."

"So he was home when you arrived? He must have been upset to see the state you were in."

"He *was* upset, but not about that. You see, I was late getting his dinner and he had a meeting. And I didn't have a salad. Those guys had ruined it."

She saw the policeman by the window look up and exchange a look with Detective Rooke, almost as if they were sorry for her. There was a short silence and then Detective Rooke went on. "And you have no idea where Sabrina and Crystal went? What might have happened to them?"

"Honestly, I haven't got a clue." *Not one that makes any sense*, she thought.

"Thank you, Andrea. You may go now." Detective Rooke smiled at her. The constable by the window turned over a fresh page in his notebook and flattened the book. What had he written about her? Had they believed her? What kind of lies had the other four girls told the police last night?

She went to the library and sat in a corner, staring blankly at *Macbeth*, act one, scene one. One by one the other grade tens came in. They whispered and stared at her. She tried to ignore them. The hands of the clock moved slowly toward lunchtime.

"Andrea Austin!"

She jumped.

"They'd like to speak to you again."

Stiff-legged, she walked past the staring eyes and back to the counsellor's office.

"Just a couple of points to clear up. You did say that you were running away from the six girls?"

"Yes. Like I told you. They caught me in the park. I had stopped to buy salad at the corner store."

"The four girls—that is, Holly, Julia, Brenda, and Meg—describe your encounter somewhat differently. They say that they were crossing the park when you turned back and began attacking them, swinging your backpack and kicking."

"But that's ridiculous! Me against six of them? It doesn't make any sense, and it's not true. They were the ones who had it in for me, not the other way round."

"Can you prove your story that the six of them ganged up on you?"

"I can prove they'd been hassling me before. In the cafeteria. Lots of people saw that. And in the science lab."

"What about in the park?"

"There were people about. Joggers, people walking dogs. Nobody helped," she suddenly wailed. "I thought with other people around I'd be okay. They must have seen what was going on. They weren't *blind*. I guess they just didn't want to get involved. Maybe they were scared too."

"You really have a grudge against the girls, don't you?"

"I . . . I suppose you could call it that."

"Especially Crystal and Sabrina?"

"Well, they are the leaders of the gang. They are the meanest."

"So you had good reason to do something to—"

"But I didn't. I did nothing. You just don't understand."

"All right, Andrea. That's all. For now."

*For now.* Her heart sank. She knew they didn't believe her. The lunch bell rang as she went down the corridor and reluctantly into the cafeteria. Nobody talked to her or sat near her—like she was contagious. Sure, she was free to eat in peace without the Six hassling her, but with the hard knot in her throat, it was hard to swallow and her sandwich tasted of cardboard and sand.

*What have those four said, Holly and the others? The police don't believe me. And the kids act like I've got some disgusting disease.*

Being picked on was bad enough. Being totally ignored was even worse.

The afternoon dragged on. She wasn't the only student who was distracted, and even the teachers seemed less enthusiastic than usual. It was whispered that everyone, even all the grade elevens and twelves, were being questioned. *Where were Crystal and Sabrina?* Someone had heard that they'd been spotted on the ferry crossing to the mainland. Someone else said that it had to do with ecoterrorists and they would be sacrificed if there was any more clearcutting. If only that were true, Andrea thought. *Nothing to do with me!*

The final bell came as a relief to everyone. Andrea emptied her locker, hitched up her backpack, and hurried out. The four were waiting outside the school wall. She turned away quickly, prepared to run.

"No, don't go, Andrea. Wait!" Holly's voice was almost humble.

"Why should I? You're nothing but grief. You lied to the police. The nerve—telling them that I attacked *you!*"

"Well, we had to say something, you know. But Andrea, what's really happened to Crystal and Sabrina? What have you done with them?"

"What have *I* done?" Andrea stared blankly. "What are you guys playing at? *You're* the ones who attacked *me.*"

"We were just horsing around. It didn't mean anything, not really. You didn't have to . . ." Holly stopped.

"I didn't have to do what?"

"Well, . . . make them disappear."

Andrea managed a forced laugh. "Do you have any idea how dumb that sounds? Is that what you told the police?"

"Of course not. They'd say we were crazy. But how else could it have happened? I saw them grab that . . . that black box of yours. Both of them grabbed it. I *saw* them. And then they weren't there any more."

"Oh, right. Sure." Andrea nodded. "That's almost as ridiculous as your story to the police that *I* attacked *you*." She tried to keep her voice firm. *Black box*. A virtual reality gizmo, she'd told herself. It couldn't be anything more. Could it?

"But it's the truth. I saw them vanish!"

"Well, I didn't, so I can't help you. Why don't you tell the police exactly what you *did* see and let them make what they can of the big mystery?" She turned away so they couldn't see the bewilderment and uncertainty that she knew must be obvious in her expression.

"Wait! You've got to help," Julia wailed.

"I don't *have* to do anything. Just leave me alone." Andrea turned on them. "Or maybe *you'll* vanish."

She ran off, but not before she saw the genuine terror on all their faces. Did they really believe that she'd made Crystal and Sabrina vanish? That she had the power to do it to them too? It would be funny if it weren't so scary.

Once around the corner Andrea slowed down to a

walk and tried to make sense of the whole mysterious affair. It all began with the maze. They'd picked it up and then . . . the rest didn't make sense. It was scientifically impossible. They couldn't have been zapped into another dimension, could they? Not in the real world, only in an SF movie. Her thoughts ran round and round in her head, going nowhere. Irrational though it might be, she could think of only one person to help her, and that was Sofia. She had given her the maze. It was the maze that Crystal and Sabrina had grabbed. In a weirdly logical way, Sofia must be the key to the puzzle. She glimpsed a downtown bus, impulsively ran after it, and caught it.

Ten minutes later she was standing outside SOFIA'S SHELVES. The painted sign creaked in the wind. The notice on the door said CLOSED. She leaned against it, her forehead against the cool glass, trying to peer inside. There were no lights in the front room. Was that a thin hairline of light under the curtain hung across the entrance to the back room? She knocked politely, waited, and then began to hammer frantically on the door.

*Please, please be there.*

No response. She was about to turn away in despair when at last she heard the key rattle in the lock. The door swung open.

"Thank goodness! I knocked and knocked! I was afraid you were away."

"Come in." Sofia opened the door wide and

Andrea followed her into the back room. The fire was lit, the kettle singing on the hob, just like before. So very ordinary, she thought, and the turmoil in her head began to subside. But would Sofia believe her crazy suspicions? Did she believe them herself? *Good question, Andrea!*

"What brings you back so soon? Are you not satisfied with the maze? Do you want to give it back?"

Andrea's mouth fell open. This wasn't a response she'd expected, and her first feeling was one of relief. "You mean I *can*?"

"That depends. If you've put yourself into it, it is no longer neutral. It is truly yours."

Andrea didn't understand any of this, but she grabbed the most puzzling word. "Neutral? How can a VR game *not* be neutral?"

"Of itself it is. It all depends on what you choose to put into it. And it is no game. Remember, I warned you to use it with care."

"I think I did." She hesitated. Would Sofia think she was crazy? "I just stepped inside and then came out again."

"You didn't go to the centre? You didn't find the stone?"

Andrea shook her head. "What *is* the stone? What is it for?"

"That depends on the intention of the finder. It can be awe-ful—meaning filled with awe—or beau-

tiful, or any number of things. But if you had no
intention, except perhaps curiosity—"

"That was it. I didn't even know what was happening, but suddenly I was inside," She paused and
went on doubtfully. "Inside somewhere . . ."

"And you didn't explore? You came right out
again?"

Andrea shook her head. "I don't understand any
of this. It's crazy! The maze is only a VR game, isn't
it? But how can it work when it isn't even plugged
into a computer with a monitor? What's going on?
None of it makes any sense!" In spite of herself, her
voice rose hysterically.

"Have a cup of tea." A steaming mug was put into
her hand. "It will calm you."

A spicy herbal aroma rose with the steam. Andrea
sniffed it cautiously and then began to sip it. Her
helter-skelter thoughts slowed down. She took a
deep breath.

"That's better." Sofia's voice was calm and deep.
"But something else has upset you—not only your
adventure into the maze."

*It's strange how easy it is to talk to this woman I've
only just met,* Andrea thought. *It's as if we were on the
same wavelength in spite of our differences. I bet she's
never heard of matrix theory.*

She plunged into her story. "It was the next day.
The Six swarmed me in the park. I had the maze in

my backpack. I wish I'd left it at home, then maybe none of this would have happened, but how was I to know?"

"Drink your tea and tell me calmly, Andrea."

She explained how, after she was swarmed, Sabrina and Crystal fought over the maze. "There was a weird smell, like a shorted circuit, like a thunderstorm. Then there was a flash of light. Could it have been lightning, do you think? But when lightning strikes, people get killed, don't they? Not . . . not *vaporized*?"

"Not as far as I know. Go on." Sofia was unsurprised, but watchful.

*Which is very strange.* Andrea frowned. *Why isn't she surprised?*

"Because that's what happened, according to the other four. There was this flash of light and I shut my eyes, just for a second, so I didn't actually see what happened. But they've gone—totally vanished! Or could the four of them be making it up, just to get me into trouble? No, that doesn't make sense. They really *have* gone. The police have been notified. The principal suggested that they might have run away, in which case the other girls *were* lying. But they don't act like they're lying, more like they were . . . well, . . . scared. Scared of *me*. And the police are really on my case, like they believe I'm involved, but I'm not. I didn't do anything, Sofia, honestly I didn't."

"I know you didn't, Andrea. What I believe has happened is much more serious than that." Sofia's face was grave, a frown furrowing her forehead. "What a catastrophe!"

"What is it? What's happened then?"

"I surmise that Crystal and Sabrina attempted to gain control of the maze while it was activated."

"Activated? What does that mean? Oh, it was hot when I picked it up. Are you saying that it *did* vaporize them? That they're gone—dead?" Andrea's hands went to her mouth and her voice shrilled out of control.

"No, no, not that serious, but it has absorbed them. They're inside the maze."

Andrea's hands dropped and she stared at Sofia and then gave an uncertain laugh. "Are you saying that the maze swallowed them up? That they're inside that little black case? Oh, that's crazy!"

"It would be if they were. No, the black box that is small enough to put in your pocket is only a simulacrum of the real world of the maze."

"A what?"

"A simulacrum. A representation. Just as a photograph or even a hologram of you is not you, but only an appearance of you."

"So where's the real maze? In another dimension?" Andrea laughed weakly. *It's all so unreal,* she thought. *If it were anyone but Sofia, I'd know they were putting me on. But . . .*

"Exactly." Sofia's face was serious, her frown deepening. "Another dimension."

Andrea's half-smile faded. "Why are you looking at me like that? Like it's my fault?"

"Your fault? Of course it's not! But when you first entered the maze, even though you were in it for such a short time, it became in a way a part of you. Then, when your safety was threatened, it reacted."

"You mean . . . you're telling me that it swallowed up Crystal and Sabrina to save *me*?"

"More or less." Sofia nodded. "Though at least one of the girls must have had a strong reason of her own for escaping this world. In any case, it is still *your* maze and it will be your responsibility to rescue them."

"What do you mean, *rescue* them? Me?"

"You must go into the maze, as you did before, but this time you must do more than wander. You must have the *intention* of finding Crystal and Sabrina and bringing them back to the real world."

Andrea shivered and shook her head, remembering the spooky grey passages that seemed to wind on and on. "No way! They can find their own way out, like I did."

Sofia looked at her intently, saying nothing.

"They *can* get out, can't they?"

"Not on their own. For them it is a trap, a dangerous trap, since it responds to their emotions in kind, and from what you have said, they are not very pleasant people. All they can do is wander through the maze until you find them. As far as family, friends, and the police know, they have indeed vanished. They are no longer in this time frame."

"Time frame? I went into the maze and when I came out, no time had passed."

"Because it's yours," Sofia repeated.

"This is crazy! I came to return the maze. Thanks for the gift, but . . . well, . . . it's been nothing but trouble. *You* know how it works. *You* can get Crystal and Sabrina out. Can't you? Please say 'yes' . . ." Her voice died at the expression on Sofia's face. In spite of the fire and the cosy room, she shivered.

There was a silence. She tried again. "Suppose I do try to rescue them and *I* get lost? What happens then?"

"It is your maze. It will respond to your will. You must have faith in yourself."

*Faith? I'm just a wimp. I don't have courage to stand up for myself at home or at school. I just let rotten things happen to me. No way can I go on this crazy rescue.* She blinked back unexpected tears.

"It hasn't been easy for you, has it? I do understand." Sofia covered Andrea's hands with her own. They were warm and full of a kind of energy that seemed to go right through Andrea's body, like a healing light. Suddenly Father's attitude, the new school, her glasses and awful clothes, even the bullying ways of the Six, seemed insignificant.

She took a deep breath. "I wish . . ." She stopped. "If only you could . . ."

"I can't come with you, you know. This is something you have to do alone. Now go home, my dear. Tonight begin to explore your maze and find your friends."

"Friends? But you don't understand—they're enemies. They only want to hurt—"

"You mustn't think of them that way. You mustn't contaminate the maze with negative thoughts. Pay attention to what I'm saying. It's vital to your safety. Keep your thoughts intent on good. I warn you, it won't be easy. It may even be dangerous. If those two girls are strong-willed enough, they will be imposing *their* personalities on the maze. You may find it is like a war. But remember, it will be a war of wills only. Be strong, and never doubt yourself."

A final pat on the hand and she was ushered out the door and up the steps to the alley. A bus was waiting and she took it almost all the way home, just stopping off to buy a salad for dinner and, on impulse, a bunch of Michaelmas daisies. Automatically she looked around, but there was no sign of the four. She realized that she'd actually scared them off. It was a good feeling, not being afraid that they'd be waiting around the next corner, threatening her. If she were able to rescue Crystal and Sabrina from wherever they were, would things be better? Or would they go on bullying her just like before? But that was a risk she'd have to take, wasn't it? She couldn't just abandon them.

She pushed all thoughts of the maze out of her head, difficult though that was, and concentrated on organizing dinner and cleaning up the apartment a bit before Father got home. He must have had a good day. He actually noticed the flowers. She'd put them in a vase on the freshly polished table in the hall, his mail stacked neatly in front.

"Your mother used to . . . but that was a long time ago. I don't suppose you would remember."

*Of course I do, Father.* She almost said it out loud. *I remember everything about Mom and I miss her like crazy.* He sighed. The moment passed and he took his mail into his study.

He liked it when she got home before he did, she realized, even if he said nothing. *Could it be that he's missing Mom?* she wondered. *Maybe he can't bear an empty house and I'm better than nothing.* She wondered why she'd never figured this out before. It didn't make her lack of social life any easier, but at least it made it understandable. *His being miserable can't last forever,* she told herself. *Maybe by the time I'm in grade eleven he'll have got over it. Or maybe he'll even meet someone else.* She tried to imagine him dating another woman and failed utterly. She wondered how he had "dated" Mom. Certainly, for as long as she could recall, there were no dinners out, no flowers, no small gifts. Mom was just *there*, seeing that meals were punctual and the dry cleaning was picked up. How dreadfully sad!

During dinner he was unusually restless, unable to concentrate on his book, as if something were on his mind. Abruptly he put down his knife and fork. "The police contacted me at the office today, Andrea. I'm sure you know why. It was a very disturbing interview. Surely you know better than to associate with the more disruptive elements at school?"

"That's not fair, Father. They ganged up on me, six against one. They swarmed me in the park. I told you that yesterday."

"The police implied that you might have had something to do with the disappearance of two of them. I trust there is no truth in this?"

"None at all, Father," she said stiffly. "The other girls in the gang said it was my fault, but they were lying. I told the police that. I just don't think they believe me."

"Hmm. So they said. I told them that my daughter was no liar."

"Thank you, Father," she answered humbly. They finished the meal in silence. Today the silence didn't bother her. Her thoughts tumbled about in her head.

*I don't want to explore the maze. I could get lost in there. Suppose . . .*

But Sofia had definitely told her that Crystal and

Sabrina were trapped inside it. It was up to her to find them.

*And what am I supposed to do then? I'll just be trapped with them, won't I?*

There seemed to be no easy answer. She sighed and Father looked up sharply, his voice accusing. "Not sulking, I hope, Andrea?"

"No, of course not, Father."

She took her time clearing the table and doing the dishes. She tidied the kitchen and polished the countertops till they shone. Only then did she go reluctantly to her room. There were assignments to be done. That took up most of the rest of the evening. She told herself that she'd wait until Father had gone to bed, so there would be no chance of interruption, before tackling the maze.

She picked up the black box with its inlaid silver top, this gift that she'd accepted instead of the amulet of which she had so often dreamed, the amulet that she had imagined would be, like her escape into books, a doorway to another and happier world.

*What is it really?* she wondered. *Two possibilities— no, three. Either it's a black box with no particular meaning, or it's magic, like the amulet or the magic ring in E. Nesbit's books. Or a simulacrum, as Sofia called it. A copy of a real maze one can actually go inside. Like a very advanced virtual reality game, driven by my own energy and emotions rather than by an external program.*

"Virtual reality," she decided out loud. "That's cool. Magic is too weird and scary."

Once she'd decided on this, she let her logical brain take over. The problem with a real maze was that you could no longer see the pattern once you were inside. The black box was only a . . . a simulacrum, Sofia had called it. If she were to copy out the design *before* entering the maze itself, it would be like having a map. She would be able to see where she was going. Carefully she copied the silver pattern onto graph paper and, once that was done, traced out the route to the centre. Left and another left, she seemed to remember from her first experience. But that led to a dead end and she had to begin again. Two rights? Funny she should have forgotten so soon.

Slowly she traced the correct path around the maze to the centre, a long elaborate path that wove to and fro, frequently doubling back and heading away from its final destination. When she finished, she folded the paper and tucked it into her skirt pocket, confident that now she would never lose her way.

Ten o'clock exactly. She peeked into the living room. Father was placing a bookmark in his book and laying it carefully on the side table.

"Good night, Father. Sleep well."

"Good night, Andrea."

Back in her bedroom, alone, there was nothing to stop her. She sat on the edge of her bed, the small black oblong in her hand. Her fingers touched the small gap that marked the way in. *It is only a simulacrum of the real world*, Sofia had said. Nothing to be afraid of. She told herself that it was indeed a virtual reality game, one that she could step out of any time she chose.

She could feel the black case with its silver tracery growing warm in her hands, inviting her in. *I don't want to go.* She took a deep breath. *But I must.* She set the forefinger of her right hand over the line that marked the beginning of the maze.

Were Crystal and Sabrina really lost inside this? Had they been sucked in? It seemed incredible, like science fiction, not real life. Would it still work if she didn't really believe in it? Well, there was only one way to find out. She took a deep breath. *Crystal, Sabrina, where are you?*

# FOUR

# CRYSTAL

Crouching behind the rhododendron bushes, her gang around her, Crystal felt the power surging up. Sometimes this feeling was so strong and wonderful that it wiped out all the pain and anger inside her. She wanted to laugh and shout, but she bottled it up inside. After all, she was the leader. She was cool. In control.

She watched Andrea scurrying along the path toward them. The kid didn't have a clue, scuttling along like a worried mouse. She looked incredibly stupid in that flowered skirt, those old-fashioned sandals, the glasses, like someone out of a 1950s video. Ridiculous. Hardly human. Insect! The perfect victim. It had looked like school was going to be really boring this year, but not any more.

The mouse was almost level with the bushes. Wait for it . . . "Now!" Crystal shouted and the six of them jumped out and swarmed over her.

Andrea reacted really fast, slipping off her backpack and swinging it like a weapon, knocking Meg and Brenda out of the game. She was quick. That was a surprise. Not such a mouse after all. Stupid of Meg and Brenda to have been caught unawares like that. They never did amount to much—just two great lumps—and were in the gang only to make up the numbers to that power number: Six.

"Get that pack!" she yelled, and Holly and Sabrina obeyed like good lieutenants, pulling it away. But the stupid kid wouldn't let go. Crystal felt annoyance smoulder inside her and flame into rage. *I'll show you, stupid.* She tripped her, a foot thrust between her legs. Andrea pitched forward and fell on hands and knees on the gravel. *Ha! Bet that hurt, insect!* But in spite of the fall, she was still hanging onto her backpack. Crystal stomped on the insect's hand. Heard the cry of pain and stored it in her memory for later. Stomped on the other hand. Now Sabrina got the backpack and the insect was flat on the path, put in her place. Where she belonged. Crying. That was more like it.

"Sit on her, you useless lumps," she ordered Meg and Brenda. "What's this?" She tossed the grocery bag to Sabrina.

"Just lettuce. My, what a nerd!" Sabrina threw the plastic bag in the air.

Holly reached up and caught it. "We'll make a salad!" She and Julia began tearing up the lettuce and scattering the pieces over the insect. She struggled and protested "Please don't!" and Crystal put a foot on her shoulders and pushed her down. This was *so* good. The six of them working together like a team. Herself in charge.

"Too bad we don't have any dressing!" Julia laughed.

"Look, this'll do for salad dressing. Sunscreen? In September? What a nerd!" Sabrina tossed the bottle to Holly.

"What else is in her pack?" Julia asked.

Crystal upended it. "Hey, this binder's really loose." She could feel the insect's body squirm under her foot.

"Please don't!" Now she was in tears. Good.

Crystal pushed her down again. "Oh, not to worry. I'm sure you can redo all this. You're *so* clever." She opened the binder, letting the breeze take the pages, one by one.

"Wait a minute. What's this?" Sabrina held up a black and silver case. It looked expensive, not in the insect's style at all.

"Give it here," Crystal ordered. "What's inside? Where's the catch?" She fumbled and failed to find it. "Stupid thing!" She dropped it on the ground and took her foot off Andrea's back to stamp on it.

"Let me look," Sabrina shouted eagerly. "I bet I can open it."

She reached down to grab the box, still under Crystal's foot. "Uh-uh. It's mine!" Crystal stooped to grab it from her.

As they tugged, Crystal felt the box suddenly grow

hot. Boiling. Almost too hot to touch. Maybe it was a bomb and she'd set off the mechanism by stamping on it. She dropped it with a gasp, but it was too late. There was a brilliant flash that blotted out the insect, still flat on the ground, covered with lettuce leaves and sunscreen. It blinded her too, so she could no longer see the gravel path, the rhodos, the blue sky above, even the park.

She could hear Sabrina scream. "I'm blind. It's exploded and blinded me." Crystal staggered to her feet, bumped into another body, and snatched her hands from her eyes to grab hold of it.

"Sabrina?" She blinked. Her eyes were dazzled with the afterglow of the blinding light, greenish ghosts dancing behind her lids. She squeezed her eyes shut and opened them again. That was better. She could see Sabrina plainly now, facing her, her eyes huge, her mouth agape.

"What's going on, Crystal? Where are we?"

Crystal's hands dropped from Sabrina's arms. She looked round. Blinked and looked again. Maybe the explosion had done something to her brain, like a concussion.

There was no park, no rhodos, nothing familiar. Just the two of them standing alone in a grey tunnel that seemed to go on and on with no end to it. She turned and looked behind her. The same grey tunnel. On and on for ever. The roof of the tunnel seemed just over their heads, but when she reached up, there was nothing—it was as if her hand went through whatever was up there. She could feel panic tightening in her throat and she couldn't breathe. She wanted to scream, but there wasn't enough air in her lungs.

Crystal hadn't choked up like this in years, not since the first time Dad beat up on Mom and stormed out for more liquor. She could remember— like it had just happened—Mom locking the door and standing with her back against it, like she was defending herself—and Crystal—against him. But it wasn't like that, was it? Mom was no heroine. She was a stupid woman with blood dripping from her nose onto her soiled cotton housecoat. Dad had begged to be let in, making all sorts of promises. "I swear I'll never lay hands on you or the girl again."

And he hadn't. Not till the next bottle. Crystal could still recall his anger, as if it burned her, like a fire consuming them both.

"I'll never let a guy have power over me like this," she'd sworn to herself. Little by little, as she grew older and stronger, she found out how to deny Dad his power over her by being as angry as he was. By sucking the anger right out of him and making it hers.

She'd seen a cool SF movie once where the alien had done just that. It was like she was a super-absorbent paper towel, blotting up the mess and misery, denying its effect.

She couldn't remember what had happened to the alien in the movie, but she became so filled with anger that sometimes she felt like a balloon, ready to explode. And if she couldn't find an outlet for it, she'd start to wheeze, like now.

Where were they? Where was this endless dreary tunnel? What had happened to the park? The other four? She needed to lash out at someone or something. But who? And how?

She forced herself to stand still as she struggled to breathe, forcing her lungs to open and fill, to take another breath. To push it out. *Take it easy*, she told herself sternly.

She hadn't choked up like this in years; she'd given up carrying a puffer, which was only a sign of weakness, she had told herself. Easy. Another breath. She wiped the sweat from her forehead. There. That was better.

She made herself stay cool. She reached out and touched the wall. Unlike the roof it felt real. Grey plastic stuff. When she stretched out both arms, she could touch either wall. She could feel the tightness in her chest lessen. She was beginning to be in control again.

"What's the matter, Crystal? Why are you choking? Oh, God, maybe it's poison gas. A bomb. Or a mine. That box—"

"Hush, Sabrina." Her voice came out evenly. Nobody would ever know about that moment of total panic, that loss of her precious power. "It can't possibly have been a bomb or a mine. Think about it. We were right on top of it. Holding it, for Pete's sake. *We'd be dead.*"

Sabrina's eyes widened even more so that Crystal could see white all around the irises. "Maybe that's what's happened to us. Maybe this weird place is where you go when you're dead. It's horrible. It's got to be Hell. And it's all your fault. I wish I hadn't listened to you. I wish I'd never been part of the gang. I wish I hadn't . . . oh . . . oh . . . oh!"

Crystal channelled some of her fear into anger. Her fingers tingled. She reached over and slapped Sabrina across the face. The hysterical screams turned off like a tap. "We are *not* dead. We haven't been blown up, so shut up and let me think."

Sabrina put her hand to her mouth. She snuffled and began to chew her cuticles. After a moment's silence she said timidly, "Where . . . where do you think we are then?"

Crystal squared her shoulders. She took a deep breath. Yes, she was in control again. Sabrina's fear only made her stronger. *I'm afraid of nothing*, she told herself. *I will get out of here, wherever here is. It's okay. I can handle it. I'm in control.* She turned and looked behind her. Or was "behind" actually the right way to go, the way they'd arrived in this place, blinded by the light? She could only guess.

She turned again. "I don't know yet, but I will. We have to explore this place. We'll go this way."

As soon as she'd spoken, she knew she was right. *It's like a dream*, she told herself. *A weird dream where we're being tested. But tested for what?* She didn't know, maybe she didn't *want* to know. She forced herself to walk briskly along the passage, action overcoming fear.

The path curved and twisted. On and on, like walking a treadmill. Suddenly it branched. Crystal stopped and Sabrina, half a step behind, bumped into her. "Oh, for Pete's sake, stop crowding me."

"Sorry, Crystal. Which way d'you think we should go now?"

"Should? Whichever feels right, of course."

Sabrina put a hand out to the wall on the right. "This way?" she suggested timidly.

"Uh-uh." Crystal shook her head. "Maybe it's okay for you, but *this* way feels better to me." Unhesitatingly she turned left. "You don't have to follow me, Sabrina, you know. You can go your own way."

"By myself? Are you kidding? I'd rather tag along with you, if you don't mind."

Crystal shrugged. "Suit yourself." Irritation surged within her. Had she really *liked* having Sabrina as her first lieutenant, as a friend? The two of them against the rest of the world? The two of them and the other four in the gang? As she trudged along the grey unending labyrinth, it all seemed meaningless, the whole of her life—meaningless.

She could feel the sides of the passage crowding in on her, stifling her, and she flung her arms out in sudden panic. Her fingers just touched the walls—it was all in her mind, then. But she *was* suffocating. The grey silence was choking her and she could feel her chest beginning to tighten again. When she was a kid she always had to have a puffer with her. She hadn't needed it since she left home. Fostering had been no fun. Mr. and Mrs. McGrath had never *loved* her. They had made it obvious that they were only doing their Christian duty by taking her in, but at least they hadn't suffocated her with pretend love. That gave her a kind of freedom, and her asthma went away.

*I don't need that puffer, not any more*, she told herself. She doubled her hands into fists until her fingernails dug into her palms. *Pain helps*, she reminded herself. *Other people's pain is best, but mine will do.*

She turned a corner, came to a further dividing of the path, and stopped abruptly. Sabrina bumped into her from behind, but Crystal didn't notice her, nor the apology that trailed off into silence. Her heart was thudding like a jackhammer. She dug in her fingernails. Ahead of her the passage was no longer grey and empty, but had widened into a room, an all-too familiar room—the bedroom she'd had as a kid. It was summer. The window was open and a light breeze was blowing the curtain. There was a row of stuffed animals on the shelf above the bed—she threw them out when she was ten, she remembered.

Sitting at the dressing table, staring into the mirror, was her younger self. Her present self stared back at the reflection of the tearless blue eyes, cold and angry, like hers today. The hair was tangled, the T-shirt a mess. No, worse than a mess. It was smeared with blood. Her arms were completely smeared with blood. In her right hand was a pair of nail scissors. As Crystal watched, her younger self dragged the points down the tender insides of her arms.

*Don't!* Crystal wanted to shout at her younger self. *It won't help. It'll just make more trouble.*

"Crystal," Sabrina whispered from behind her. "Is that really *you*?"

"Don't you say a word. Not one word," Crystal hissed. "That was long ago. Another life. Not important." She crossed her arms, feeling through her shirt the fine silvery scars of her long-ago anger and defiance. She was right. It hadn't helped. Mom had gone on being a victim. Dad had gone right on being a drunken bully. All that had happened as a result of her self-mutilation was a boring session with a shrink who seemed to think *talking* would help. As if it ever had . . . "Don't hurt her, Dad, please don't!" And "Why don't you stand up to him, Mom? We could leave him. Yes, we could." Words. Useless words . . .

She turned resolutely away from the bedroom—she hadn't thought of that room in years—and from the defiant, blood-smeared child, denying them both. Instantly the grey passage was back. It was as if that interlude had been a bubble in time. Nothing more. Not real. Crystal strode down the grey passage, refusing to look back. "Stupid kid," she muttered.

"What did you say?" Sabrina looked back over her shoulder. "Why, the room's gone. *She*'s gone."

"She was never there," Crystal snapped. "She was only in my mind." She opened her fists and stared at the red crescent marks on her palms where her nails had dug in.

"But I saw her."

"Forget it, Sabrina. I mean that. I don't know what it was, but it never happened." Denying it made it less terrifying. She didn't have to tell Sabrina how true that image had been, as if this place had the power to suck memories out of her head and make them real. "Come on. Let's get out of here."

"Like, do we have a choice, Crystal?"

Crystal turned to stare at Sabrina. She was quite bright, her second-in-command, she acknowledged grudgingly. She wouldn't have picked her otherwise, would she? *Do we have a choice?* she asked herself. *We can't go back and change the past, can we? Like maybe get a different set of parents. Choice would be a fine thing!* "Oh, come on!"

When the passage divided once more, she again picked the left branch. This time she was not so deeply shocked when the greyness dissolved into a view of the McGrath kitchen. *A trip down memory lane*, she thought bitterly. Then a scary thought crept into her mind: *They say a dying person relives her whole life. Is that what's happening?* She swallowed panic and tried to look calmly at the scene unfolding before her.

Eating in the kitchen was supposed to be "homey," she remembered. Also less demeaning for the cook, who was Lucinda McGrath, so she didn't have to run to and from the dining room, serving them. It was different from home, where there was a proper dining room then, with Mom rushing apologetically to and fro, cooking up meals that were supposed to please Dad, but which somehow always seemed to end in disaster, so that every meal became a shouting match.

It had certainly been different at the McGraths' home. In the McGrath kitchen everything was in its place. The counters were clean, dirty dishes out of sight in the dishwasher. Everything was under control. That was the first thing she noticed when the McGraths began fostering her. And they never fought. Every issue, however small, was talked through until she was so stunned with boredom that she gave up and just nodded. And everyone said how excellent the McGraths were, a perfect jewel in the whole fostering system. Crystal was in junior high then. She'd learned to keep her mouth shut, to bottle up the anger growing inside her. That was when she began to gather the other five around her.

The McGrath kitchen, exactly as it was then, in

every detail, was brought to life in this grey passage. With a shiver she found she was looking at the back view of herself. A long-sleeved shirt hid the recent scars on her arms. Other scars were even better hidden. She stared past her teenage self at the motto, cross-stitched by Lucinda McGrath, framed in oak by her loving husband to match the cupboards, and hung on the wall opposite the window. A HAPPY KITCHEN MAKES A HAPPY HOME it said, with sunflowers.

*They haven't a clue*, thought Crystal now, despising the even, quiet voices, the flat minds that never soared, never reached out. *You were always so boring*, she found herself remembering, and wondered if one day she could sit down at the kitchen table with these stupid, well-meaning folks and tell them the history of the Six—explain how she had been able to reach out and find those girls she could control. Meg and Brenda were the weakest and the easiest. Hardly worth the effort, they'd come like moths around a flame, dazzled by her power. In Holly and Julia she could recognize a small part of herself. Julia needed to manipulate; Holly was spiteful and prickly like her name, needing someone to direct her spite. A bit like Crystal herself. And the McGraths had no idea.

There were red geraniums on the windowsill of the McGrath kitchen, and below them the row of Tupperware containers, with flour, rice, sugar, everything tidily in its proper place. No surprises in the McGrath home.

Like Sabrina. No surprises. Sabrina craved the kind of power that Crystal wielded, but she didn't have the savvy. She could have made it in the academic world if she'd wanted to—she was as bright as that insect, Andrea Austin. She'd once offered to help Crystal with her math assignments. *Help me?* Crystal boiled at the memory. She'd soon put a stop to that idea. She wasn't going to be beholden to any of them. *She* was the boss. *She* was in charge. What she needed she would take by force, or else not bother. Anyway, who cared about high marks?

"Boring," she said out loud. "Look at the two of them sitting there. Frozen moments. What a joke!" She laughed, hoping her attitude would convince Sabrina. "Come on. Let's go."

"Did all this really happen? Like this? Why *you*?" Sabrina caught her arm. "Crystal, are you *making* this happen?"

"Maybe." It was as likely an explanation as any. After all, she was the strongest. *Her* mind. *Her* memories. "Sure. That's what's happening. I'm in charge."

But Sabrina was getting stronger now that she'd got over her initial fear. If Crystal wasn't careful, she could take over. Better to offer her the opportunity.

"You could make it happen your way if you wanted. Why don't you go ahead?" She smiled coolly.

"You mean I could be in charge if I wanted? How would I do that, Crystal?"

"By taking the turning that feels right for you, next time there's a choice."

"Can I do that? Yeah, okay. I want to go right."

"Be my guest." Crystal spread her hands, noticing gleefully the hesitation returning to Sabrina's face. That was what it was all about, the power, the difference between taking and being given.

"I'll . . . I'll do it. Next time the path divides, I get to choose. Okay?" And when the opportunity came, it was Sabrina who led the way. "You *are* coming too, aren't you?" She hesitated.

"Sure, if you want. Whatever." Crystal shrugged as if it didn't matter one way or the other. No way she would let Sabrina guess how afraid she was, or how much she hated having her secret past replayed in living colour. She wouldn't let that happen again if she could prevent it. No way. She had never once taken the gang home to the boring misery of the McGraths. Maybe there was something in Sabrina's past, something to balance against the picture of Crystal scoring her arms with scissor blades, or even sitting in the smug misery of the McGrath kitchen, though what Sabrina could have hidden in *her* past she couldn't imagine. Dullsville was where she came from.

As these thoughts raced through Crystal's mind, she noticed that the greyness of the passage was slowly changing. Nothing dramatic. The walls became a misty green. The oppressively hanging roof seemed to grow higher. She could feel her chest relax; she was not so choked up. Hey, this was better! But it wasn't her world, was it? It was Sabrina's. That wasn't so good.

Her foot kicked something and, looking down, she saw a small branch. And there was gravel. Sabrina called out triumphantly. "It's okay. Look, there are the rhodos. And I can see the pond way in the distance. It's all right, Crystal. That's what I wanted. To go back. I've found the way out!" She walked quickly forward. "And there's the gizmo out of Andrea's pack. Look over there, on the path."

Crystal saw the black and silver box lying innocuously on the gravel. *Something's wrong with this picture*, she thought, and instinctively drew back. Where were the scattered sheets out of Andrea's binder? Where was the backpack itself? The other four? And Andrea herself, a prone insect on the path, covered with torn lettuce and sunscreen? There was nothing there but the case. It lay there, a black and silver oblong, a trap, like a land mine, waiting to explode when they touched it.

"There's the gizmo—weird!" Sabrina ran forward and bent down to pick it up. In an instant Crystal saw exactly what was going to happen.

"No! Don't touch it!" she yelled and ran forward, snatching the case away from Sabrina.

*Just as she had done before.*

She let go. Sabrina let go. The case clattered to the ground. But it was too late. In a whirling, sickening second, the gravel path, the bushes, the park, the comforting blue sky were all blotted out. They were back inside the maze.

Only it had changed. Where before it had been an unrelieved grey, now on either side of them was a hedge, like the hedge of a real maze, except that this one was constructed of knives and scissors, tightly wedged and interlaced together, so that nothing could penetrate them. It glittered menacingly.

Crystal drew back, her arms crossed, her hands automatically feeling the long-ago scars. Why had this happened? What was this place trying to tell her?

Beside her Sabrina wailed, "This is horrible! It's worse than before. How did we get here?"

"You fool!" Crystal turned her anger on her. "Why did you have to pick up the case again? Didn't you see it was a trap?"

"You picked it up too." Unexpectedly Sabrina turned on her. "It was you as much as me, same as it was last time. And I've got nothing to do with scissors and stuff. Not like you." Her voice was priggish, self-righteous, like a McGrath voice.

Something inside Crystal snapped. She caught Sabrina by the shoulders and shook her hard. As she did so, she could feel her fear changing to anger. Sabrina was crying now, begging her to stop. But she didn't want to. Why should she? It was a good feeling. Then she saw a glowing red light flicker on the glistening knives in the hedge and looked up to see a sky that seemed to be on fire. She dropped her hands and stared up. Sabrina pulled back and rubbed her arms.

"You don't have to be so mean. It *was* your fault too." She looked around and wailed. "Oh, let me out of here!"

Crystal itched to slap her senseless. She could feel her hand twitch, her arm tense. But it seemed that bad things followed her anger. She took a deep breath. *Cool it*, she ordered herself. Was it her imagination, or was the red of the fiery sky less intense?

"It's okay. We'll find the *real* way out of here. That wasn't it."

"But we saw the park."

"No. Don't you understand yet? The others weren't there, nor Andrea and all her stuff. It wasn't the real park. It was a trap. A stupid joke."

Sabrina shivered. "Okay then, smartie. If you know it all, why don't you tell me whose trap it is? Whose joke? Who's really in charge?"

*Good question.*

"We're in charge," she said at last, after a silence that threatened to go on for too long. "We can choose whether to go back or forward. Left or right. Come to that, I suppose we could just sit here and wait to see what happens next, if you'd rather do that."

# FIVE

# ANDREA

Andrea sat on the edge of her bed, the black and silver box on the table beside her. She didn't dare pick it up. What activated it? What had sucked her into the maze? If it had. *Can this really be happening?*

Sofia's words came back to her. "When you first entered the maze, even though you were in it for such a short time, it became in a way a part of you. Then, when your safety was threatened, it reacted."

*Weird. Was she telling the truth or kidding me? The bright light was real. And Crystal and Sabrina did vanish. Could the maze have swallowed them up to save me?*

*I didn't ask it to,* she protested now. *I never asked to get into this mess. It's not my fault.*

She remembered Sofia's stern face at her whining excuses. "It is still *your* maze and it will be your responsibility to rescue them," she had chided Andrea.

*I can't. I don't know how. I'm scared. It's not like a game anymore. Not like my dreams of a magic amulet giving me my three wishes.*

Andrea sighed. Life was so different from dreams—she had found that out when Mom left, when Father sold the house and she had to go to a different school.

"Your responsibility," Sofia had said.

*So I guess it's up to me to make my own future. Not dreams, but for real. Starting now.*

She took a deep breath and picked up the maze from the table, feeling its heat grow in the palm of her hand.

*Be strong, and never doubt yourself,* Sofia had advised.

"Okay, let's go," she said aloud. "Crystal and Sabrina, where are you?"

At once she felt the horrible sense of being outside her own body, of being twisted, realigned, and set back inside. Giddy and nauseated, Andrea put her hands out to steady herself and found she was touching smooth walls on either side. She opened her eyes onto the familiar vista of a grey-walled passage. *It worked! I'm inside the maze again!* She reminded herself to take the first turn to the left. And then? Was it the next right? She dug in her skirt pocket and found the piece of paper that was her map.

Feeling much braver with the map of the maze in her hand, she set off. The walls were made of some plastic substance that was smooth and cool to the touch, and the floor was so silent to walk on that she couldn't hear her footsteps—in fact she couldn't hear anything. There was no odour and the air was still. When she looked up it was into a greyness that deepened to a never-ending black—a nothingness—that made her as giddy and afraid as if she were peering into eternity. After one quick glance, she did not look up again, but concentrated on the path ahead of her.

She came to another fork in the passage. A choice. Should she go straight ahead or turn to the right? She consulted her map, paying no attention to her feelings, which, in any case, she didn't trust, not in this place, where the never-ending greyness and silence were doing funny things to her head. Right turn it was. She took it and walked on briskly.

Grey passage unfolded into grey passage. The very sameness and silence was making her jumpy. After a while she began to feel that at the next branch in the passage she would see something, *something* different, whether it would be frightening or welcoming she didn't know, but it never came. There was just more "nothing," and the nothingness made her even jumpier. She forced herself to walk on.

Was it her imagination or was the light growing brighter? The greys began to shimmer as if they were reflecting something just out of sight. She walked faster, the paper clutched in her hand. Surely by now she must be at the centre of the maze? She stopped. Ahead of her was a blank wall and a single path that led her, without any choice, around the maze and straight back to the entrance.

With no warning, it was over. There was the same horrible sensation of being pulled out of her body, somehow turned inside out and then put back, expelled from the maze, thrown out. Giddy and nauseated, she reached out to clutch at something and found herself sitting on the edge of her bed, holding the black oblong.

Her clock radio blinked at her. 10:33. Her journey seemed to have taken no time at all. Had it been a dream? Or was it real? Either way it was a failure. She'd seen nothing, achieved nothing.

This whole time thing was weird. She frowned, trying to work it out. If Crystal and Sabrina were trapped inside the maze, why hadn't they popped straight out again, as she had just done? She felt as if she'd been wandering through those grey passages for hours, but, in fact, it had taken no "real" time. If Crystal and Sabrina were still in there, wherever "there" was, why hadn't she seen them? They'd been gone for over twenty-four hours of real time. They hadn't popped out as she had done, so *where were they?*

Were they trapped in the maze, in some place hidden from her? Or perhaps they had found the centre of the maze, whereas she hadn't. The stone at the centre. Perhaps it was a secret way through to some other world—like in *The Story of the Amulet*.

She peered down at the silver line that scrolled around the top of the black oblong. She traced the path she had drawn on a scrap of paper. It was this she had followed to where the centre should be, only she could see now that it wasn't. The silver pathway looked nothing like the map she had copied and so carefully followed. She stared at the network of lines. They were nothing like her map. Maybe the passages weren't defined—maybe they could change at will. "You're nothing but a cheat," she said aloud.

Then another thought flashed through her mind. *And so are you, Andrea Austin. Thinking you could get a free trip to the centre of the maze with a map. It's like cheating on an exam.*

And anyway, she had no reason to believe that Crystal and Sabrina *had* found the stone at the centre of the maze. It was every bit as likely that they were still wandering hopelessly through the grey passages. *If I really want to find them, I'm going to have to go into the maze totally unprepared, as they had been. Take the same risks.* With a sudden lurch in her stomach, she thought, *Maybe I'll lose myself forever inside the maze, like Crystal and Sabrina.* She swallowed panic.

"Okay, I'll do it," she said out loud, to convince herself. "But not tonight. I've got to think about it and come up with a plan that doesn't involve cheating. I have to figure out how not to get totally lost." And she wondered if she could in some way mark the paths she took, like Theseus, who used a ball of string to find his way out of the labyrinth, once he had slain the dreaded Minotaur. Maybe crossing off the paths that were dead ends would be more effective than getting tangled up with balls of string. Felt markers would be great, she thought as she brushed her teeth, only she didn't have any. Or perhaps lipstick would show up even better on that shiny plastic floor, only she didn't own a lipstick. She must be the only girl in Abbotsville High who didn't. Makeup was one of the things that Father absolutely refused to allow. Then she remembered the one she bought in Kmart last year, not long after Mom left. She tried it on once. Father had pounced and said never again. It must be somewhere, lying about.

*Tomorrow*, she promised herself as she climbed into bed. *After a good night's sleep, I'll get everything organized.*

But sleep eluded her. Behind her closed eyes Andrea saw metre after metre of grey passage unfolding ahead of her plodding steps. When she finally drifted into a world of uneasy dreams, it was to relive the swarming in the park and the police interrogation.

She woke to hear Father banging on her door. "Andrea, I'm waiting for my breakfast. And you're going to be late for school."

She sat up and looked groggily at her alarm clock. She gasped. "I must have forgotten to set it. Coming!"

As she scrambled into her clothes, all the horrors of the day before rushed back at her. The black and silver oblong sat accusingly on her bedside table and she quickly stuffed it into a drawer. *I wish I'd never found you*, she thought. *You're bringing me nothing but trouble.*

*Not fair*, another part of her brain told her. *It saved*

*me from a swarming, didn't it? Those kids were mean enough to really hurt me. And now they're gone. Maybe they deserve what they got—whatever that is.*

She pushed that thought aside and ran into the kitchen. Father was waiting in the dining room, a familiar look of impatience on his face, and a sudden gust of anger swept through her. Just for once, couldn't he get his own breakfast? He wasn't stupid. Or helpless. She pushed her anger aside. Anger was a waste of energy. *But he's got to learn that I'm not a stay-at-home Mom, nor a servant.*

She glanced up at the kitchen clock, grabbed orange juice from the fridge, and poured each of them a glass. Between gulps she told him, "Sorry, Father. I'm really late. There's cold cereal on the shelf there. Milk in the fridge. And fruit. G'bye."

Without giving him time to react, she snatched up her jacket and backpack and tore out of the house.

All the way to school she was buoyed up by an unfamiliar exhilaration. *I told him. I really did!*

A small cautious voice inside her answered, *Yeah, but you'll be sorry for it when you get home this evening.*

*Maybe I can make up for it by cooking something special for dinner.*

*Why should you?* The other voice challenged her. *What do you have to apologize for?*

But this conversation between the rebel and the docile daughter was forgotten as soon as she got to school. Instead of having to elbow her way through the crowd, space seemed to open up in front of her. There was no one hanging out near her locker. In silence she dumped her books and took what she needed for the morning. She could hear the hum of voices as she went into her first class, but the voices trailed off into an awkward silence, and it was obvious that they'd been talking about her before she came in.

There was nothing about Crystal and Sabrina in the morning's announcements. The sight of their empty desks made her feel guilty. Andrea forced herself to look away. She took a deep, steadying breath. Somehow she was going to have to get through this day. Then she could go home and explore the maze. Even its possible dangers would be more welcome than the icy silence and suspicion that seemed to surround her here. And her own sense of guilt. *My maze. My fault.*

*If they just leave me alone, I'll get through the day,* she promised herself.

Then came the message over the intercom, jarring her so that her pencil dropped and rolled across the floor. "Andrea Austin, please report to the counsellor's office."

*Again.* She got to her feet and walked out of the room, her legs wobbly, everyone's eyes drilling into her back like bullets. *What now?* She knocked cautiously on the counsellor's door.

"Come in, Andrea. Sit down."

She took a deep breath and sat, facing the same

two officers, trying not to look guilty. *I've done nothing wrong,* she reminded herself. "More questions?" She tried to make her voice strong, but it came out squeaky.

"Are you surprised, Andrea? You *were* the last person to see Crystal and Sabrina before their disappearance."

"That's not true! I didn't even see them go. I've told you again and again. They were in the park, all six of them. The other four must have seen them. They can't have—" Her voice broke and she cleared her throat. "They can't have vanished." She tried to sound convincing.

"Tell us what happened."

"But I've already explained," she cried out, suddenly impatient. "Over and over. It's . . . it's persecution."

"Just once more. And there's no need to shout."

"Sorry," she muttered. "Like I said, I was face down on the path, with Meg and Brenda sitting on me. Then Julia and Holly tore up the lettuce I'd just bought for Father's dinner and they scattered it all over me. Then they poured sunscreen over me."

"Why?"

She stared. "Why? To be mean, of course. Crystal had already stomped on my hands." She held them out. They were still puffy and bruised.

"That must have made you pretty mad, huh?"

"Of course it did. It hurt. Crystal just ground my hands into the gravel."

"Why didn't you try to get away?"

"With those two lumps sitting on me?"

"Exactly where were they sitting?"

"One on my legs. The other on my shoulders. I don't know which was where. I couldn't see."

"Were they still there when the other two girls scattered lettuce and lotion over you? I can't visualize it."

Andrea frowned. How exactly had it happened? Holly had said, "Out of the way, you two, unless you want to get splashed." Meg and Brenda got off her back and grabbed her hands. Then Holly began to shake the sunscreen over Andrea's head and shoulders. She explained this.

"And then?"

Then Holly yelled something and let go. I realized that nobody was holding me down any more. I couldn't believe they were just letting me go, but I didn't stop to ask. I just got up, grabbed my stuff, and got out of there."

"You went straight home?"

"Yes."

"Your father said you were late and he was waiting for his dinner, but instead of getting it, you went straight to the bathroom and showered. Later that evening you cleaned the bathroom and did a load of laundry."

"Of course I did. I was covered with lettuce and sunscreen. The bathroom was a mess and so were my clothes."

"Only sunscreen? Or maybe you were in a hurry to get rid of incriminating evidence? Like bloodstains, for instance."

"Bloodstains?" She stared, open-mouthed. "Of course not. It was the sunscreen. Sticky lotion all over my dress. I was afraid the stain wouldn't go away if I left it."

"Your friends had vanished, but you were only interested in laundering your clothes?"

"You're twisting everything I say. It wasn't like that. I didn't know they'd vanished—that's your take on what happened. And they're *not* my friends, I told you that."

"Better not keep emphasizing that fact, Andrea. It's not wise."

"If you're trying to scare me, it's not working. What am I supposed to have done with Crystal and Sabrina? Made them vanish into thin air before going home to make Father's dinner?" She gasped and bit her lip. *Close to the truth. Be careful, Andrea.*

Silence followed her explosion. The two officers looked at each other. "Very well, you can go now. But I must warn you, if you've been interfering with a police investigation in any way, such as by hiding evidence or lying, you are guilty of a crime."

"I haven't. I'm not," Andrea managed to blurt out, hoping she didn't look as guilty as she felt. But how could she possibly explain to these two officers the brilliant light that had, somehow, in the face of all reason, swallowed up the two girls?

As she walked slowly back to her classroom, she realized sadly that she couldn't really count on Father to stand up for her. More interested in his own comfort and peace of mind, he had unthinkingly sacrificed her. He didn't mean to, she told herself. It's just that he lives in a different world. The mystical mathematical symbols that revolved in his mind were all that mattered to him. *But he did tell them I wasn't a liar*, she reminded herself.

*What will the police do now?* she wondered. *Will they examine the clothes I was wearing? Will there be traces of sunscreen even after laundering to support my story?* Then she remembered with despair that there had been blood on the palms of her hands from the gravel that scraped them when she fell on the path. Some of the blood had smeared onto her clothes when she brushed off the lotion-soaked lettuce.

*That's all nonsense*, she told herself. *They were just trying to shake me up so I'd tell them what happened to Sabrina and Crystal. It doesn't mean they believe I'd hurt them.* She went into English class and tried to pay attention to the guilt problems of Lady Macbeth, which seemed trifling in comparison to her own.

The morning crept by. English was followed by math, then the lunch bell. She ate her sandwiches alone in a corner of the cafeteria and thought how ironic it was that only a few days ago she would have been thankful to be able to eat in peace without being hassled. Now she just felt horribly lonely.

After lunch she had a spare, which gave her more time to worry. She had intended to do the advanced math that Mr. Canton had set, but found herself staring blankly at the page instead.

*If I'd done badly in my assignments when I first came to Abbotsville High, then maybe Crystal wouldn't have been jealous and they would have left me alone.* She sighed. Not true. There were her glasses, her stupid skirts, her lack of makeup, and her general air of nerdishness, which were more than enough to label her as victim even without the added insult of being top of the class in math.

*So now I'm a threat,* she thought. *I wish I could just be normal.* She promised herself that when this nightmare was finally over, she would change. She would stand up for herself at home, somehow get hold of decent clothes, get rid of her glasses, and stop doing absolutely everything for Father. *He can afford a housekeeper,* she thought. *But why should he bother when he's got me as a slave?*

The last class was biology. *Well, at least I don't have to worry about Crystal or Holly doing something gross again, like putting my dissected frog in Ms. Williams's desk,* she thought as she carefully labelled the drawing she began last session. She could tell that Ms. Williams was still unfairly mad at her for that incident. The temperature dropped every time she came by Andrea's seat.

Finally the last bell went and she was free to go

home—to face the maze again. Even thinking about it, in the ordinary open air, with the sun shining down, gave her a chill. Suppose she were to vanish like Crystal and Sabrina? There would be no one to rescue her, no one to realize that the secret lay in the innocent-looking black box. Perhaps she should write a note saying where she was, but to whom should she address it? Certainly not to Father. Definitely not to the police. In the end, she gave up the idea as stupid. It would just land her in the funny farm when it was discovered. If she were still there, that is, and not lost in the maze.

The familiar pattern of the evening unfolded. Cooking dinner. Eating in stony silence, broken only by the sound of Father turning the pages of the book he brought to the table. He was still mad at her for not stopping to cook his breakfast. She sometimes thought that a screaming match would be preferable to silence, but that was not Father's style. She loaded the dishwasher, tidied the kitchen, and went to her room to tackle her unfinished assignments. Finally they were done and she had no excuse.

Reluctantly she took the black oblong from under the T-shirts in her drawer. Remembering the plan she had devised as she lay awake the night before, she hunted for her long-abandoned lipstick. It wouldn't be in any obvious place like her purse or the top drawer of her desk. After some thought, she found it in a cardboard shoe box hidden at the back of her closet.

Here she had stored a collection of mementoes, all totally useless but too precious to throw out. She picked them up, one by one. The program for her junior high graduation. That had been fun. She'd actually had a partner and they'd danced together and she'd had a good time. There was a ticket to a rock concert that Mom and a friend had taken her to, just before Mom left. Father had read the review the next day and got on Mom's case all evening, but it was too late then. Andrea had already had the best evening of her total life and nothing he could do could spoil it.

Other things in the shoe box had lost their significance. Why had she kept a blue marble streaked with white? And a fine embroidered white handkerchief? But when she lifted it, there was a faint waft of scent, and memory stirred uneasily. Had it been Mom's?

Down at the bottom of the box was the cylindrical lipstick case. She twirled it open. A most unthreatening pale pink, yet Father went ballistic when she wore it. She smeared it against the back of her hand, wondering if it had dried up totally. It left a faint smudge of rose as her skin warmed it. It probably wasn't much good, but it would have to do. She dropped it into her skirt pocket and, on sudden impulse, stuffed the cotton handkerchief over it.

She looked at the black and silver box on her bedside table. How was she going to enter the maze this time? How was she going to find Crystal and Sabrina? Perhaps by imitating them. She tried to remember the muddled seconds before the flash of light.

"What's this?" Sabrina had held up the box and Crystal had grabbed it from her. She tried to open it, then failed and dropped it on the ground and stamped on it. Sabrina had reached down, said something . . . and then it had happened.

*Stamp. Grab.* She picked up the box and imitated the moves. Nothing happened.

What had Sofia said? A kind of warning? *Take care. Have the right intention.* Crystal and Sabrina certainly hadn't had that. *Stamp. Grab.*

Anger and greed. That's what it had been about. But Sofia had warned her to take care. She certainly wouldn't be taking care if she were to imitate their negative emotions, but how else was she going to find them?

*Oh, heck! Go for it, Andrea!* It was halfway between a sob and a prayer. She thought of anger, of power, of greed, as if she *were* Crystal. She grabbed the box as if she were snatching it from someone. And it worked! She felt the heat, the wrenching sense of being displaced, of being turned inside out and then reassembled. Like in *Star Trek.* "Beam me up, Scotty," she muttered, though there was nothing funny about it. Nothing to joke about, she thought as she opened her eyes. She gasped.

She had been transported not to a familiar world of grey tunnels, but to a place completely different and bizarre. It was like a maze built outdoors, as in the garden of some European great house. She'd seen pictures somewhere. But these hedges defining the walls of the passages were not made of green yew or privet, smoothly clipped and beautiful, but of shining knives and scissors, so densely intertwined that she could not see between them. Were they real? She cautiously reached out to touch and drew her hand back quickly from their razor-sharp edges. They were real all right!

A murky glow in the sky was reflecting off the shining blades. Looking up, she saw, above the steel hedge, a sky lit up as if it were on fire. She took a step forward and her feet felt, not the smooth plastic of the "other" maze world, but something rough and unpleasant. She looked down. Beneath her feet was a wiry mat of dry grass, interspersed with thorns, flat rosettes whose spiky leaves seemed to reflect the spiky hedge.

With a grimace Andrea realized that she had been successful. This was no safe, boring, grey passage, but a place dangerous and menacing. Without doubt she had found Crystal's and Sabrina's world. Her guess at using Crystal's emotions to enter Crystal's maze world had been right. This is what Sofia's warning had meant. *Take care. Have the right intention.* But to find Crystal and Sabrina, she had to follow Crystal's anger. She shivered, looking at the glistening knives. What anger!

She had no map to guide her. She was as helpless as if she were sailing on an unknown sea in a leaky boat without a life jacket. She took a deep breath and dug her hands in her pockets. Her left hand found the small cylinder of lipstick, and she remembered her plan, small and feeble, but nevertheless a plan. With lipstick in hand she set out. She might not have a life jacket, but she did have something like a compass on this journey into the unknown.

At the first fork in the path she came to, Andrea chose to turn left. She hesitated. She had been counting on having smooth grey plastic walls and floor to mark with her lipstick. Obviously it would be useless on the thistly ground cover, so different from the grey plastic floor she had counted on. To mark one knife blade out of thousands didn't seem particularly helpful, but it was the best she could do. She picked an extra prominent blade and marked it with a single slash /. If she came to a dead end and had to turn back, she would know that the particular passage had been explored and she would then mark over the slash to make a big X. It wasn't much of a plan, but it gave her a small feeling of being in charge.

Ahead of her a flame suddenly shot across the path. She gasped and stopped abruptly. She waited and watched. Nothing happened. But when she moved slowly forward, it happened again. It was obviously triggered by her approach. She moved back a pace. *Swoosh*, like a dragon's breath. She ran forward as fast as she could, feeling the heat against the back of her legs, seeing the scorch marks on the spiny grass and thistles.

Was the whole route mined with booby traps like this? Was Crystal's anger leaving a trail of such violence? Her heart thumped and she wiped sweat from her forehead. Sweating with fear? No, she really was getting uncomfortably warm, as if she were approaching whatever conflagration was reddening the sky above. In the distance she could hear a rumbling roar. Was it thunder, or the crackling flames of fire?

She walked cautiously forward, keeping an eye out for more surprises like the unexpected flames. When she came to a division in the path, she again picked left. She looked for a particularly noticeable knife or blade in the hedge, but nothing was especially prominent. Would she even notice a pink smudge of lipstick? The hedges of knives and scissors reflected the redness of the sky. Digging her hands in her pockets she discovered the map she had made on her previous expedition. She tore off a small scrap and impaled it on the thorn of a thistle. When she looked back she could see its whiteness glimmering against the sombre dark green of the ground cover.

Flashes of what seemed to be lightning lit up the

metallic hedge and reflected off the blades of knives and scissors, temporarily blinding her. She automatically reached out her hands and recoiled as she encountered the brutal sharpness of the hedge. *Ouch! That hurt!* She looked down at her fingers. Small beads of blood oozed from the tips. This place was real, not some incredibly advanced virtual reality game. She sucked her fingers and tasted real blood. A person could get seriously hurt in here! A person could die.

It took all the courage she could muster to move cautiously forward, expecting at every move to encounter another burst of flame or something worse—things she was desperately afraid of, like snakes. Or scorpions. She told herself not to think of such things, that thinking might make them happen. She came to a dead end and had to retrace her steps. Her plan had worked. There was the scrap of paper. And there was the mark on the steel hedge. She completed the X and took the other path.

She began to feel sure she was on the right track now. The rumbling of thunder was definitely closer, but now it was recognizable. It wasn't thunder at all, but the sound of two people quarrelling. She couldn't make sense of the words, for they were distorted as if the speakers were at the bottom of an elevator shaft or in a huge, echoing building.

"Crystal!" she shouted. "Are you there? Sabrina, is that you?"

She waited. The sounds went on. They were definitely human voices. She yelled again, "Crystal! Sabrina! It's Andrea. I've come to help."

There was sudden silence. So they *had* heard.

"You're there. I know you are. Keep talking. Maybe I can find you and together we'll figure how to get out of here."

*Silence.*

"Please listen to me. You don't understand. You're trapped in here. You've been missing for days. You've got to trust me. I'm only trying to help."

Help . . . Help . . . Help . . .

Was it just an echo? Or was it Crystal's voice mocking her? A cascade of hysterical laughter echoed through the murky passages, surrounding Andrea so that for a second she found herself with her hand to her mouth, as if the sounds had come from her.

She tried again. "Crystal, is that you? I want to help."

The sound of a slap was brutally close. The flat of a hand very hard against a cheek. Then silence.

# SIX

# CRYSTAL

Sabrina shivered. "Stay here? With these horrible knives and scissors?" Her voice rose. "No way! I want out of here."

Crystal shrugged. What difference did it make? This was some sort of nightmare they were trapped in; this didn't have anything to do with logic. Where was her power now? *Gone.* Rage rose inside her, hotter and hotter, till she felt like a volcano ready to erupt. She raked her nails down the inside of her arms.

She licked her dry lips and tried to swallow. "Don't be a crybaby, Sabrina. Virtual reality, that's what it is. Neat effect, but not real. Why, I bet I could put my hand through it."

"Oh, Crystal, don't!"

She paid no attention to Sabrina's warning, but recklessly punched out a hand, determined to give the lie to whatever was happening to them. Her fingers smashed into solid steel and she pulled her hand back with a gasp. "Yikes, that hurt!" She sucked her fingertips and shook her hand. Drops of blood fell on the grass and it, too, began to change, grow harsh and saw-toothed, studded with prickly thistles.

Crystal stared in shock at her fingers. *But I'm the one who chooses*, she told herself. *I'm the one to decide if I'll hurt myself or the other guy.*

"Who are you?" she yelled at the steel hedges, at the sky above. "You've got no right to mess with me!"

As if in answer, the sky began to turn a dusky red, like the reflections of a fire.

"Stop it, Crystal!" Sabrina screamed. "You're losing it!"

"Stop what, stupid? Losing what?" Crystal's hands doubled into fists. She could feel her rage grow and grow.

"Don't you see? *You're* doing all this. You're making it happen. It's not fair. It's supposed to be my turn. Like . . . like *my* life. Not a bit like this. Not knives and fire. It was nice and peaceful. Safe." She began to sob.

"Well, well, crybaby. Let the real Sabrina Collins come out! Is this what you're really like inside? If so, I don't want you in the gang any more."

"And maybe I don't want to be a part of it. I wish I never was."

Crystal gave a hard, humourless laugh. "Good. Go ahead and leave. And we'll see just how you make out with the rest of grade ten. They'll despise you, that's what. Without me you're nothing but a boring, middle-class, fat zero."

"I am not. I can make friends on my own."

"Really? Like you did when we were in grade seven? Remember? You were a lost little puppy till I took you on and made you my special friend."

Sabrina bit her lip. Crystal saw it quiver. Saw more tears gather in the large blue eyes. She could feel laughter bubbling up inside her, could feel her power returning. She shrugged off the stinging pain in her fingertips. That was nothing, not with the power beginning to zing through her body again.

She gave another stab. "So, d'you want to leave right now? Off you go then. If you don't like this scenario, if you think it's all my fault, tough! Go ahead and make a world of your own if you can. And go ahead and find your way out of here."

It was almost too easy, hardly worth her skill. The tears overflowed, running down the stupid kid's cheeks. Sabrina blubbered, "No, I didn't mean it. Don't leave me on my own here, please. Crystal, you can't."

She wailed and Crystal grabbed her, putting her hand over Sabrina's mouth. "Shut up then, crybaby! You can tag along, but no more crying. I can't stand it, okay?"

Crystal strode along the knife-edged passage, came to an intersection, and turned right. A flame shot out suddenly across the passage at ankle level, and she stifled a scream and jumped back. "Watch it!" Amazingly, she managed to keep her voice level. "Boy, this place is really playing games with us!"

There was a fluttering in her chest like moths trying to get out. She could almost see them—big, velvety-winged brown moths with fat, furry bodies—like the ones at the summer camp they'd sent her to that year when Dad was in the money. It had been even worse than she had imagined, with Hitler-type females screaming at them from morning till night.

"You'll like it and it'll be good for you. You and your loud mouth just make matters worse between your mom and me. A bit of discipline is what you need . . ."

"Now hold it," she'd yelled. "You're using my summer vacation to *discipline* me?" Isn't school enough? I won't go and you can't make me."

"You'll listen and no more mouthing off," Dad warned. "Unless you want me to take my belt to you."

She knew that they could make her go, that she had no power at all. That was bad enough, but then she found the coach tickets when she was looking through Mom's purse for some spare change. They were planning a jaunt to Las Vegas while she was being warehoused at some summer camp from Hell. For her own good! She tore the tickets into confetti and strewed the pieces over their bedroom floor, but it was only a gesture. He slapped her on the side of the head till her ears rang, and the tour company issued new tickets.

Dad drove her to camp. Neither of them spoke till he dumped her and her bag in front of the main lodge, where the flag was flying. "You'll be sorry," she yelled as he drove off, his tires spinning, showering her with gravel.

It was like an army camp. The only good time was in the cabin at night when it was quiet, with no more screaming from the Hitler-types. Just the one kerosene lamp on the table by the window, and moths, hundreds of them, trying frantically to get in.

Right now, in this nightmare maze, she had the horrible feeling that if she were to open her mouth, the moths she could feel fluttering in her chest would come flying out. She shuddered and covered her mouth with her hands.

Sabrina didn't seem to notice anyhing. Her hysterical babble filled the silence. "Maybe we'd better go back, Crystal. Those flames—they're like blowtorches—they could burn us up. Or something else will. Maybe napalm. It's like this place is angry at us. Let's go back to where it was all grey and peaceful. Maybe we can find the park again—the real park. I promise not to touch that black box."

Crystal swallowed the imaginary moths and took her fingers from her mouth. "I told you before, the park isn't real. It was just a trap, like a hook with a worm wriggling on it. You swallowed it."

"I said I wouldn't again. Though maybe I'd rather find that park and sit under a rhodo bush and wait."

"Wait for what, dummy?"

"For something to happen, I guess. For all this to be over."

"Nothing's going to happen until we make it happen. I thought I'd made that clear to you. You're not going to find any power by sitting under a stupid bush. You won't find anything. Is that what you really want? If so, just go back. I don't care, only don't expect me to come with you. I'm not about to spend my time under a dumb rhodo bush!"

Her voice rose. She could feel anger and power coming back, and the memory of that terrible summer camp. She remembered how she felt when she'd got back at those sadistic so-called counsellors on the last night of camp, when it was too late for them to punish her, except by sending her home, which was where she'd be going anyway.

She could still remember the moment of pure joy when she'd leaned through the window of the counsellors' cabin and tipped over the lamp so that the kerosene spilled and ran across the table, and flames licked up and caught the curtains. For an instant she was scared at what she'd done. She never thought they'd catch fire so quickly. Pretty stupid to have flammable curtains in a summer camp.

She was back in her bunk by the time they ran

screaming out the door. They'd never have found out who did it if it hadn't been for that snivelly little kid—the one who wet her bed every night and cried for her mommy. Crystal had threatened to break the arm of any kid who told that she'd been out of the cabin that night, and they'd all kept mum, knowing she meant it, all except for the snivelly kid. Sometimes people could surprise you.

Here in the maze world flames were licking across the murky sky just like the flames that had devoured the curtains in camp. There was a growl of thunder, a long way off. *Great effects*, she told herself sarcastically, psyching herself up. Or maybe she was talking to whoever was in charge, whoever—whatever—it was that was running the show. She walked forward and another flame shot across the passage, higher this time, maybe at calf level.

"Okay, Sabrina," she yelled. "Run for it before it can charge up again!" And she ran quickly past the danger point and turned. Sabrina was cowering on the far side. "Look, it's okay. Come forward slowly. Then when it's done its thing, run for it." She tried to keep her voice calm.

"I can't, Crystal. I'm too scared."

"Then you can stay there forever, for all I care. But it's not going to get any better while you wait. So come on, run for it!" she ordered.

She watched Sabrina screw up her face, shut her

eyes tightly, and run forward blindly. The flames roared. "My legs!" Sabrina gasped. "Look, I'm burned!"

"Your jeans are a bit scorched, that's all. You're okay, so stop fussing and come on." She strode forward. The passage branched again. Left or right? Did their choice make any difference to what happened? Or was it all predetermined so that what she chose didn't make a bit of difference?

"Go on. You choose." She turned to Sabrina. "Make it your world if you can."

"I could if you'd only just stop." Sabrina turned on her.

"Stop what?"

"You know, anger, memory. Whatever's in your head that's making all this happen."

Crystal stared at her. *Was* she running the show? Was this all *her* doing? The knives? The sky? The fire? That was ridiculous. She gave an uncertain laugh. "If you don't like it, Sabrina, you go right ahead. Make something different."

"Maybe I can." Sabrina stood still, shut her eyes, and took a deep breath. "I'm going to imagine that rhodo bush back in the park, where it's all peaceful and unscary. I'm going to sit under it until all this is over, so there!"

# SEVEN

# SABRINA

Slowly the red faded from the sky. The hard bright-
ness of knives and scissors softened to the greenness
of a hedge. Under her feet was grass. Sabrina took a
deep breath.

*I can do it*, she thought. *I can be my own person,
make my own world.* She walked on slowly. Away
from Crystal's overpowering anger it wasn't that
difficult. Only—the hedges wavered and began to
glint with steel again—*only not to be afraid. That's
important.*

She took a deep breath and imagined the air was
scented with greenery. "It's like when I was little,
and we went to visit Gran and Gramps on the farm.
It was so green, so peaceful." Sabrina walked on,
telling herself that around the next corner, or the one
after that, she would come upon the park again.

And there it was, just as she had willed it. Not the
real park, of course, as it was hours ago when it all
began, when they swarmed Andrea. This park
seemed empty. Holly and Julia, Meg and Brenda
were gone. No Andrea either.

Sabrina sat under the largest rhodo bush and crossed her legs. Long ago she had taken yoga classes with her mother at the Y. *One of Mom's futile attempts to boost my confidence, to think for myself,* she remembered. *Not too effective. Poor Mom. Well, maybe it's not too late for me to change.*

Now, sitting with her back straight, her hands in her lap, she gazed up through the dense leaves at the glimpses of blue sky above. The small puffy clouds were as motionless as if she were looking at a painting. She thought about junior high and this, the first year of high school. She thought about Holly and Julia, Meg and Brenda. Crystal? *No, I won't think about her. She might still be strong enough to suck me back into that nightmare world of hers. How was I conned into the gang? To become Crystal's friend? No,* she realized. *I was never her friend. I don't think she has any friends. We were just puppets. Or pawns. And I was the worst, the most slavish.*

For a moment Sabrina felt a gush of self-pity, and the too easy tears flooded her eyes. She straightened her back and blinked. *Stop that,* she told herself firmly. *I've escaped her world. I'm as strong as she is.*

"You've got to learn to stand on your own two feet," Mom had said, not once but many times. "You'd want your dad to be proud of you, wouldn't you?"

But words alone hadn't given her a backbone. Not

even the memory of a war correspondent father, killed in some scuffle in a far-off land with an unpronounceable name. So brave in the face of danger. A hero . . .

*Not like me. I did try, Dad, honest I did.*

"Wake up, Sabrina, and pay attention," a teacher would snap, with some joke at which the class would laugh. Then, in spite of her efforts, the tears would start again.

She had been miserable until Crystal chose her to be part of the gang, setting her apart from the rest of the class, until Crystal showed her that anger dried up tears, that bullying transferred the helplessness to the other guy.

Sabrina moved suddenly, rubbing her hands over her face. *I was horrible,* she remembered. *Not just to Andrea, but to other miserable kids in junior high. Kids like I had been. I guess I hated them for having the same weaknesses, for being small and worthless. I wasn't going to be like them, no way!*

She sighed and looked up at the sun. The clouds hadn't budged, not by a centimetre.

*When I get out of here, it'll be different,* she promised herself. *I'll try and make friends with the other kids in class, like Andrea maybe.* They had a lot in common, she realized. Both of them were basically shy and good at math. Maybe Mr. Canton would let her join the advanced math class if she pulled up her marks and worked hard. She could make friends that way.

Sabrina sat beneath the unmoving rhodo bush and promised herself that she *would* be different, that she *would* change, starting now while she waited. Then, once she got out—if she got out—it would be into a new world.

# EIGHT

## ANDREA

Andrea had a vivid mental picture of Crystal standing, not so very far away, on the other side of the impenetrable steel hedge, her arm around Sabrina, her hand clamped over Sabrina's mouth, muffling her hysterical sobs.

"How am I going to help you if you won't let me?" Andrea called out in despair. She listened, but there was only silence. She waited and slowly became aware that the maze was changing. The hedge of knives and scissors was blurring, becoming more green. The harsh thistles under her feet were softening into short grass. The red faded from the sky.

Green surrounded Andrea, and she felt wrapped in peacefulness. Unhesitatingly she walked along the hedge-lined path until it widened into a park, and she glimpsed blue sky dotted with cotton ball clouds.

Framing this tranquil view were the dark, coarse leaves of a huge rhodo bush and beneath it, almost at Andrea's feet, Sabrina sat cross-legged on the ground, her face as still and calm as a stone Buddha's.

"What are you doing here?"

Sabrina looked up and smiled. "Hello, Andrea. How's it going? This is really your place, isn't it?"

"The maze is mine, yeah. But this—it's like the real park, but not quite. Nothing's happening, like it's frozen."

"There was *too* much happening in there." Sabrina nodded toward the shadowy passage behind her. "It wasn't mine—all Crystal's—so I left. Escaped actually. Looking for somewhere peaceful. So I guess this little bit of the park *is* mine."

"But what are you *doing* here?" Andrea asked again.

Sabrina lifted her hands from her lap and dropped them again. "Just waiting."

"Waiting for what?"

"For all this to be over. For Crystal to stop fighting. Something like that."

"I don't understand."

Sabrina stared. "But it's *your* maze. You've got to know what's going on."

Andrea shook her head. "Not really. Only that you two got sucked into it, and it's my job to find you both and get you out if it."

Sabrina smiled. "Well, you've found me."

"You're not scared, are you? When I heard you in there . . ." Andrea remembered the raised voices, the crying, the slap. "You're okay, Sabrina?"

"I am now. Once I got away from Crystal, it all

began to make sense. I've been sitting here in my quiet place, working it out."

"That's amazing. You've . . ." Andrea hesitated over the right word, the tactful word. "You're not like Crystal any more."

"The gang, you mean. No, that was a really dumb move. I was trying to take a shortcut to popularity—being noticed, being in charge, not being scared any more. Crystal made it seem so simple. If I were part of her gang, I'd have it all, no problem." She looked straight up at Andrea. "I'm really sorry. I behaved disgustingly to you. If—no—*when* we get out of here, I'll try and make it up to you."

"You can start right now by helping *me* understand. I've been running so hard to keep up that I've not had time to work out what makes the maze tick." Andrea sat down beside Sabrina. "I guess you're safe here in your refuge, but Crystal's another matter altogether. She's one step ahead, and I don't trust her." Andrea remembered the knives and fire and gave a sudden shiver. For an instant the sky darkened and there was a distant rumble of thunder.

"Watch it," Sabrina warned. "Evil, anger, they're always just around the corner."

"Sorry." Andrea struggled to push the images of anger out of her mind.

"Crystal's hugely strong," Sabrina went on. "I don't know a lot about her—she's very secretive—but I guess she's had a pretty horrible life, and she's put on a kind of armour—does that make sense?—to protect herself. She's got two weapons, pain and anger. I'm guessing that everything you saw back in the maze was Crystal fighting her demons. Oh, it's hard to put into words, but that's the most sense I can make of what happened back there. I had to get out. She was practically killing me—the part of me that's any good, that's worthwhile."

"Oh, boy! And I've got to go back and find her—fight her on her territory and with her rules. How am I ever going to do that?"

Sabrina listened in silence, her hands folded in her lap. Her eyes were closed. After a while she opened them again. "The maze says . . ." She stopped. "Hey, that sounds weird! I guess it *is* weird. The maze is telling me that you can't destroy whatever Crystal is making in there. She's too strong and anyway, fighting her on her terms would use the wrong kind of energy, the bad kind, *her* kind. You've got to *change* Crystal's images into something less harmful, something other than what she is trying to do. Is that any help?"

Andrea tried to smile. "Maybe, I guess. I'll try anyway. Wish me luck. I'll see you later."

"Later? There's no time here, Andrea. Haven't you noticed? The clouds don't move. No one's going by."

Andrea tried to grasp the concept of frozen time. "When I go out of the maze it's as if no time had passed. But outside, you two girls are definitely missing. Weird. So, I guess, you're not getting tired sitting here, thinking?"

Sabrina smiled. "Tired? Oh, no. It's very restful. Don't worry about me."

"I'll see you, like, any time."

"Peace!"

"Yes. Thank you, Sabrina. I'll keep it in mind." She got to her feet and turned back reluctantly to the green tunnel of the maze.

# NINE

# CRYSTAL

Crystal looked around. Was the hedge softening? Was the sky less ruddy? No way. Sabrina didn't have that kind of power. She blinked and stared. Where *was* Sabrina? Where did she go? Suddenly she was alone. Abandoned?

"No way! I'm in charge here," she yelled, and the flames shot out. The sky roared and the ground shook. She shut her eyes. *No, I didn't mean it. Not like that. I don't want to go back to that world. I want to go somewhere different, some place where there are no stupid people from my past, reminding me.*

The ground shook under her feet and she staggered and regained her balance. She opened her eyes. The knife-edged hedges were gone. The maze was gone. She was alone, as she had wished. She turned. On all sides was a pathless jungle of weird-looking trees, ferns, and dense, leafy growth. She sank to her knees and dug her fingers into the ground. It felt so real, it was amazing. Mucky and damp, smelling of decayed vegetation.

There was a rumbling sound. Thunder? She

looked up. Above the dense trees she glimpsed a cloudy sky. Over to her right was a faint reddish glow, nothing as savage as the angry fire she seemed to have evoked in the maze. For want of any better choice, she decided to explore in that direction, and began to push her way through the trees, over fallen logs, around giant ferns. A dragonfly blundered by, backed up and hovered. Crystal's hands went up to protect her face. It was huge. Unreal. As big as a seagull. Bigger. She'd never seen a dragonfly that size before. She shuddered and frantically batted it away.

As she struggled through the undergrowth, she slowly became aware that the sky was growing lighter. The ground was rising and soon she could see, beyond the tangle of vegetation, of creepers and waving fronds, a serrated range of mountains ahead. One of them glowed red, smoke billowing from its top. A volcano. There was a sulphurous stink in the air and the ground shook beneath her feet. Suddenly she recognized the place. She'd been here before— but how could she have been? It didn't exist in the real world, did it?

Not now it doesn't, she realized. But millions of years ago it did. It was exactly like the diorama of life in the Cretaceous era that she'd seen in the museum. Back in the everyday McGrath world. It was the sort of useful thing they did on weekends— going to museums.

*This is too much*, she thought. *Any moment now a dinosaur will come stomping through the trees.*

"No!" she shouted aloud. "Forget I thought that!"

How loud her voice was. And how total the silence that replaced it. She strained her ears, hoping even for the whir of the monster dragonfly's wings, but there was nothing. Even the mountain had quietened down. Nothing. Nothing.

*I'm alone.*

The thought persisted relentlessly. *Alone.* She steadied herself against the smooth trunk of a slender tree. *I asked to be alone, didn't I? And the maze listened. But I've always been alone, haven't I? Or have I?* Faces whirled through her memory—Mom, Dad, the McGraths, kids at school, the gang. Of course she wasn't alone. That was stupid, wasn't it?

*But I've always been alone inside. Is this any worse?*

The answer was there, cold and definite. *Sure it is. In this world you really are alone, Crystal Newton. You don't exist at all.*

She could feel the blood drain from her face. It was hard to breathe. Where was her puffer? Her chest was full of brown furry moths, fluttering. She sank to her knees again, her fingers clawing at the mud.

*It's like being dead*, she thought desperately. Then she thought, *maybe that's better.* She found herself wondering curiously why, in all the times she'd cut herself, she had never done herself a serious injury, never really risked herself. Why?

*Because I'm afraid of dying,* she realized, and gave a humourless laugh. *Caught between a rock and a hard place, Crystal Newton. So what are you going to do now?*

*Not give up.*

It was a small thought, no more than a seedling sprouting somewhere deep inside her, but it was enough to bring her slowly to her feet, steady herself against the tree trunk, and look around her again.

Between the jungly growth and the burning mountain she could catch the occasional glimpse of something shining—a lake, maybe—reflecting the red smoky sky. She set off determinedly in that direction, stumbling occasionally, steadying herself against trees, trying to quell the jitter in her stomach.

Gradually she was able to push the fear aside and nurse her anger, blowing on the embers of it within herself. *It's all Andrea's fault that I'm trapped here. She's spooky—a witch—trying to get back at me. It's not my fault. None of it's my fault. They've all got it in for me—teachers, the McGraths, Mom and Dad. Everyone hates me, but that's okay. I hate them, every last one of them.*

She reached the edge of the lake, a muddy, shallow beach all torn up and eroded, with deep footprints sunk into the mud. Huge footprints, the size of plates. So big that she didn't at first recognize them as footprints. When she did, she looked around uneasily for their makers, listening, straining her ears. Something that big would make a lot of noise. There was nothing. It was very still. With her arms crossed, she waited and began automatically to scratch at the old scars. Pain drove out fear. Pain and anger.

The ground trembled again. Was it an earthquake? Or the approach of a very large animal? She turned and saw Andrea standing staring across the lake. How had she found her way here? Had she been in that other world, the one of knives and scissors? Spying?

*It's not her place, it's mine. She's got no right to be here*, she thought angrily. In the same instant she saw, behind Andrea on the slope, a tree trembling, wavering, and then falling, crushed beneath the feet of a creature so enormous she could hardly take it in. It was more like a building walking—walking towards her. Or perhaps it was stalking Andrea. Andrea was closer to it. If she could get Andrea to move instead of just standing there, then the creature would certainly notice her first.

It was weird. Crystal realized that her body was frozen. She couldn't move to save her life, but her mind was working at double speed, like it had done before in interviews with counsellors and police. For a long moment she stood there, fighting to overcome her fear.

*I can beat it*, she told herself. *And get rid of that*

*stupid Andrea at the same time*. She forced herself to move, to find a stone, to throw it. She broke through the barrier of fear that froze her, bent forward, and groped for a stone. Her fingers closed around one, lifted it, and hurled it so that it would land right in front of Andrea. *That'll get her attention*.

It worked perfectly. Andrea turned. She didn't look particularly surprised. In fact, she seemed almost relieved. "There you are, Crystal. I've been searching for you everywhere. Let's get out of here, shall we? It doesn't look too healthy a spot." Her voice was steady and Crystal couldn't help being impressed. It was almost as if Andrea was in charge. But she wasn't, was she? Behind Andrea the great head, with its rows of jagged, flesh-tearing teeth, turned slowly, ponderously. Crystal's eyes were fixed on it, willing it to look at Andrea and then to react. Crystal felt a hysterical giggle bubble up inside her.

"This is a horrible place you've found. Let's go!" Andrea stood there, as much at ease as if she owned this place, not knowing that it was all Crystal's. *Her* invention. It was obvious that she was totally unaware of the monster behind her.

Crystal's fists clenched. She could feel the nails biting into her palms. *Come on, stupid,* she urged the huge dinosaur. *Move it! Come on, pea brain. Get going*. She waited silently, standing very still, waiting for the moment to begin running—to escape.

"What is it, Crystal? What are you staring at?"

Andrea turned and her voice choked at what she saw. For an instant she stood and then she ran. Improbably, she ran uphill, toward the beast. For an instant Crystal thought she'd gone crazy. Then she understood her strategy as Andrea ran right past the monster, close enough to touch the hind leg that rose like an enormous tree trunk beside her. She ran by it and out of sight.

*You're not stupid, Andrea,* Crystal thought grudgingly.

For now the monster's head moved slowly back toward Crystal.

# TEN

# ANDREA

Andrea reluctantly willed herself away from the green peacefulness of Sabrina's world into some other place, a world of Crystal's making, a world of anger and disorder. It was not too difficult to do. It was almost as if Crystal had left a trail behind her, like ashes and the smell of burning. All Andrea had to do was follow her destructive path, which was not difficult, only terrifying. Where was Crystal leading her?

*I don't want to go.*

*But you must. It's your responsibility.*

*I'm not in charge any more. It's not my maze. I don't want any part of her world.*

*It's only in her world that you're going to find her.*

*I don't have any power, not there.*

*Yes, you do.*

*Not her kind of power.*

*No, your own. You have all you need. Trust yourself.*

Andrea bit her lip. *Okay, okay. I'm going. Don't nag*, she told her other self. She closed her eyes in concentration, caught hold of the crimson thread that was Crystal's anger, and began to reel it in.

The ground trembled beneath her feet. She felt a humid warmth against her skin and smelled decaying vegetation. *Crystal, are you here?* She asked silently, and felt, in an instant response, a wave of anger like a hot flame wash over her. *Oh, yes. She's here all right!*

She opened her eyes on a world that contrasted startlingly with the rigorous simplicity of the grey passages of the original maze. Grey, orderly, unimaginative. *Is that a reflection of my personality, of my emotions?* she wondered. *I wasn't always like that—when Mom was still at home.*

The bizarre hedges of knives and scissors and the flashes of flame were reflections of Crystal's psyche, but Crystal was changing—and not for the better. There had been a sort of order, even to the flame throwing. *This world is entirely different*, she thought. Instinctively she knew that it was savage, primeval, a place without order.

She looked through a tangle of dense jungle, of strangely unfamiliar trees and ferns out of some nightmare, toward a range of distant hills where black smoke and glowing lava spilled from a volcano. Above her the red sky reflected the savage cataclysm below. The ground shook again and she steadied herself against one of the strange-looking trees.

Below her glistened a wide lake or a sea, its water reflecting the turmoil of flame and smoke that reddened the sky. *She's down there*, an inner voice told her, and she set out, following what seemed to be a trail marked by broken branches, gouges in the peaty soil and uprooted ferns. *Something big came this way*, she told herself. *The size of a tractor, but not a tractor. Obviously not a tractor.*

Andrea paused to look around. It was very still. There was no wind. She couldn't see far through the trees. Almost anything could be lurking in there. The ground trembled again. An earthquake? Or possibly a very large animal moving toward her? She listened, heard wood snap, and began to walk as fast as she could downhill toward the water. It looked refreshing and she felt suddenly thirsty, but when she got closer to it, the smell of rotten eggs was nauseating and she changed her mind and stood, hesitating.

Again the ground trembled beneath her feet. Across the water the glow of the volcano seemed to intensify. She *should* be safe at this distance. Even a lava flow would cool before it reached her, wouldn't it?

*Crystal, where are you?*

Something landed, *plunk*, in the decaying vegetation at her feet. She looked up, imagining something like a coconut palm shedding its fruit. No, it wasn't a palm tree, only something like it. So what had fallen so close to her? She looked down. A stone lay at her feet, *thrown, not dropped.*

She straightened up and turned. There was Crystal, watching her intently, not moving.

"There you are, Crystal. I've been searching for you everywhere. Let's get out of here, shall we?" she called.

Crystal stood as if she were frozen, staring at her. Hadn't she heard her?

"This is a horrible place you've found. Let's go!"

Still Crystal didn't answer. There was something peculiar about the rigid way she was standing, as if she were waiting for something to happen. And now Andrea noticed that she wasn't actually looking at her, but past her, staring as if she were hypnotized.

"What is it, Crystal? What are you staring at?" Andrea's voice trailed off into silence as she looked over her shoulder and saw where Crystal was looking. For a moment she couldn't take in its hugeness. Legs like tree trunks—only trees didn't have wicked claws like giant parrot beaks. A chest the size of a house. She craned her neck upward toward the tree tops and recognized, like a cliché, like a bad joke, the wide mouth, the ranks of pointed teeth.

With a chill she knew where she was. In the Cretaceous era. Alone. Except for Crystal. And *Tyrannosaurus rex*.

She choked and swallowed. Stood frozen, waiting. The great head turned slowly from where Crystal stood rigidly at the edge of the lake to where she, Andrea, had stopped, a stone's throw away from the monster. Then she realized, in a flash, what Crystal had planned. A savage response in a savage world. *She wants the beast to go after me!*

*But I'm not your enemy*, she wanted to protest, only she knew her protest would be useless.

Instinctively, before the eyes in the great head could focus on her, she turned and ran, not away from it, where it could see and follow her, but toward the monster, counting on the fact that she was so very small, so far down among the undergrowth that she might not be noticed. Speed and smallness were her only defences. She ran toward the nearest leg. It was like an enormous tree trunk. She could have reached out and touched the wrinkled skin, as tough as tree bark. She ran past the great tail that balanced the creature's huge neck and head like a counterweight. Then she raced up the hill, along the trail of crushed bushes and fallen saplings, the bulldozed path of the dinosaur.

She yelled as she ran. "Come on, Crystal. This way," with no idea whether Crystal was following her or not. And where did "this way" lead?

She dared not stop until she reached the top of the ridge. Only then did she pause to catch her breath and look back. Beyond the water, the mountain and the sky above it were brilliant with burning lava. She could no longer see Crystal. She had no idea where her adversary was or what she was doing. So far she had failed. What else could she do but run away?

Crystal had tried to kill her—indirectly, but still, death by dinosaur.

Her legs gave way and she slid down till she was sitting with her back against a small tree with pretty fan-shaped leaves. She closed her eyes against the red sky that seemed to reflect Crystal's anger, in the same way that the flame throwers and the ruddy sky in the maze had. In her mind's eye she could still see Crystal staring—not at her, but at the monster dinosaur behind her—staring as it approached Andrea, willing it to see her and react, saying nothing. She felt the stone that Crystal had thrown, still in her hand, felt the muck of a long ago world.

"But it's not real," she said out loud. "The dinosaur's not real, is it? It's all Crystal's invention. Crystal's world." A world of consuming anger. A world with no other humans. Had Crystal deliberately defined this prehistoric place, or was it the doing of the maze itself, translating the emotions it picked up in any way it sought fit? As if this other world were a mirror of Crystal's psyche?

*Get us back to the grey passages, to the exit,* she told the maze, but nothing happened. *I'm not strong enough. Am I even strong enough to escape Crystal's world?*

The ground shook and the distant volcano glowed menacingly. Remembering Sabrina's advice, she tried to swallow her own anger, to quell the voice screaming inside her: *She tried to kill me back there.*

She managed to will her anger away, telling herself that she forgave Crystal, that Crystal didn't know what she was doing, that her unthinking anger was the engine that was running this extension of the maze, that was making all this happen, as Sabrina had deduced.

Andrea gave a big sigh and pushed her hands against the ground, ready to get up again, to struggle on as long as she had to. To her surprise there was no longer a mass of wet decayed leaves beneath her, but smooth dry plastic. She opened her eyes cautiously and saw to her relief that the savage prehistoric world had vanished. In its place were the grey walls and floor of the original maze world.

She got stiffly to her feet and walked back to the entrance, through the twisting turmoil of the changing dimensions, and into her familiar bedroom. There were the ordinary sounds of Father in the bathroom, brushing his teeth with unnecessary vigour, rinsing his mouth and spitting emphatically into the basin, as if he were getting rid of a day's contamination from the outside world.

She blinked and looked wonderingly around her familiar room, which suddenly seemed strange— almost alien. She pushed open her bedroom window. In the distance was the faint wail of an ambulance. She took a breath of cool air. Twenty-first-century air. The moon was rising. Would it have looked the same back then? She drew back into the room and stared at her very ordinary hands, hands that had dug into the muck of sixty-five or seventy million years ago, now perfectly clean. And where was the stone that Crystal had thrown at her, that she had picked up? Back there, she supposed. Along with the dinosaurs and volcanoes.

She pushed the images of disorder and anger from her mind and gave herself a mental shake. That was Crystal's place. It was Crystal's choice to stay in that savage and primeval place rather than come back with her.

Not a surprise, really. Crystal despised her and all she seemed to stand for. *But Crystal doesn't know what it's like to be me. Maybe if she had, she wouldn't have picked me as her particular enemy.* Too late now. Crystal was trapped in the maze, which reflected her anger and pain.

*I've got to go back and find her. I've achieved nothing, except for finding out that Sabrina is okay, that she's no longer an enemy.*

"Peace," Sabrina had said.

*It wasn't just a salutation,* Andrea realized. *It was advice. If I can't keep anger out of my own life, anger at Father—yes, and at Mom too—how can I possibly help Crystal?*

Father knocked at the door. "Good night, Andrea."

She opened the door. In his shabby dressing gown—she must try and persuade him to buy a new one—he seemed suddenly lonely and vulnerable. Part of her wanted to reach out and hug him, but another part held her back. *He'd be startled out of his mind if I did something as unexpected as that,* she thought.

"Good night, Father."

"You . . . you look tired. Get a good night's sleep."

"Yes, you too." She reached past her exhaustion and gave him a big a smile in lieu of a hug. He turned and shuffled down the passage.

*A good night's sleep.* Time to try and forget the nightmare and go to sleep, hoping that it would give her the strength—and the courage—to face another day of school, and another night of searching the maze. Only how many paths were there? Into how many worlds would she have to venture in pursuit of Crystal?

She got ready for bed, memories of sharp-edged hedges, of flames, volcanoes, and savagely toothed dinosaurs swirling around in her head. Maybe tomorrow she would find Crystal and bring her home.

Maybe.

# ELEVEN

# CRYSTAL

Crystal felt the anger boil up inside her and grow and grow till she imagined it blowing out the top of her head, as if she were a volcano. How dared that insect Andrea get the better of her! *If I could just get my hands on her I'd show her . . . I'd fight her every-where!* Her fingers stretched out like claws and her nails tore into the dirt, which was no longer the oozy leaf mould of a prehistoric swamp, but greasy clay. She opened her eyes and stared into darkness. No forest, no volcano, and probably no dinosaur. Where was she?

A sudden flash tore through the darkness and blinded her. There was a screaming noise overhead followed by a deafening explosion that shook her body through and through. Somewhere to her right a shower of dirt rose into the air and spattered down. Instinctively she ducked and found herself cowering in what seemed to be a deep, mud-filled ditch. The air was filled with a terrible sweet-sour odour of decay.

Where was she? Back in the maze? She looked around. No grey plastic-lined tunnels. No green hedges nor hedges of knives and scissors either. It was a little lighter now, or perhaps her eyes had adapted to the dark. She found herself edging along a platform of duckboards set above squishing, stinking mud. It was some kind of trench, the walls on either side dug out by hand, scraped out of the same mud. On her left she could see where an explosion had gouged away a section of wall, leaving a cascade of dirt. Above and beyond the wall looped tangles of barbed wire. The trench angled to the left and meandered on.

There was another flash and another scream overhead. Her ears rang with the explosion. Dirt spattered on her head and shoulders. "Where am I?" she yelled. "What is this place?"

*You asked for war,* a cool voice inside her head answered flatly. *And war is what you've got.*

"But not *this* kind of war!" she screamed at the red sky. A rocket shot upwards and blossomed into a white flare that illuminated the maze of trenches where she crouched. She ducked and covered her head. The white light lit her like an actor on a stage. Out there in the darkness a thousand eyes could be watching her. "It's *her* I want."

*And what'll you do when you see her? Throw mud pies?*

"No! I need . . . I want . . ." She stood up, regardless of the explosions around her, her arms flung out, unsure of what she really did want. But suddenly she was holding a gun, the kind she'd seen in movies and on news flashes. It must have weighed a tonne, and her arms sagged under the unexpected weight.

"Okay!" She took a deep breath, heaved it to her shoulder, and pointed it across the tangle of barbed wire. She pulled the trigger and felt the recoil bruise her shoulder. Pain, yes! But it was worth the pain. All she had to do was to continue shooting until she got that insect Andrea, or until she ran out of ammunition.

"Are you there, Andrea?" she yelled recklessly. "I'm waiting for you." She pulled the trigger again.

"I'm right here." Andrea's voice sounded close, too close, not out there beyond the barbed wire. Crystal whirled round. *So the enemy is here.* She stared into the twilight, but could see nothing but muddy walls. She fired and mud exploded and spattered her face.

"Where are you? Come out where I can see you!" She loosed off another round. She thought she saw blood blossom on the trench wall and she forced her anger one notch higher. "I've killed you, insect, haven't I?"

"That's not blood. Look again, Crystal."

Before her eyes the red was becoming flowers, a whole field of them, opening scarlet petals to the sun. The sun rose and in the blue sky a bird sang sweetly.

"No!" Crystal screamed. "It's not supposed to happen this way! Stop changing things!"

"Put the gun down," the calm voice said.

*How come Andrea isn't angry? This isn't how it should work. Andrea's supposed to fight back. One on one. That's how it should play out.*

She forced aside the bewilderment, the uncertainty. It was still *her* choice. She, Crystal, was still in charge. She always would be. So maybe she wasn't going to confront Andrea on the battlefield. Okay. Maybe that wasn't a good scene. Too impersonal. Not really satisfying. But if they were to meet each other one on one, like in one of those old Western movies . . . Hero and villain facing off each other on Main Street, U.S.A., pacing slowly toward each other down the deserted street, fingers splayed, ready to reach down and grab the trusty gun from its holster. *Yes, that's the way it's got to go.*

Crystal chuckled. *Yes, I'm stronger than she is. I'll show her.* The weight of the Kalashnikov disappeared from her arms. In its place she felt the heft of the belt slung around her waist. Her hand moved and touched the gun sitting in its holster on her hip. *Yes, this is better. Far better. This is so good!*

She willed the muddy trench out of existence. In its place was the scene from that old movie—what was it called?—*High Noon*, that was it. *Only I'm not the reluctant hero, Gary Cooper.* She imaged a dusty street stretching ahead of her, lined on each side with a row of wooden buildings.

Overhead the sun sucked the land dry. Something

scuttled across the street in front of her. In a flash her hand was on the gun, whipping it out of the holster, blazing at—at a tumbleweed. Just a dried-up tumbleweed. *Hey, I'm in charge here.* She challenged whatever was running the worlds of the maze. *This is all mine!*

*So where is Andrea?* Somewhere in this scenario she knew her enemy must be lurking. Crystal squinted through the sun dazzle at the false fronts of the wooden stores, at the upper windows, and at the shadows of the saloon porch. Silence. Nothing moved except for her own shadow stretching away in front of her. *It's not supposed to play out like this.* Andrea should be walking down the dusty street towards her. Her anger against Andrea's. Anger feeding on anger.

"Come on, Andrea. Where are you?" she challenged. "Come out, you coward. Show yourself!"

Something white, like a handkerchief, fluttered from one of the upper windows of the saloon. She caught a whiff of fragrance, like flowers—like lilies-of-the-valley—and with it the unfamiliar memory of loving kindness.

A hated voice. "Listen to me, Crystal."

"That's not my memory!" she screamed. "It's yours. I don't want any part of it. You've got no right interfering in my world."

"My world too, now." It was the same quiet voice she'd heard on the battlefield. Its reasonableness drove her crazy. She clenched her fists. The voice droned on. Somehow it reminded her of the McGraths. "I got you into this mess, though I didn't mean to. So it's up to me to get you out. But you've got to help me. I can't do it alone."

*Alone.* The word drifted out across the dry road like a piece of tumbleweed.

Crystal hesitated. Not to be alone. To have a friend. It was a terrible temptation. But it would mean giving up the fine independence she'd fought so long to hold onto. To have a friend would mean sharing herself. Giving up her hard-won privacy. Giving up her anger. It was far more than she was prepared to sacrifice.

*Alone? I don't care if I am alone. This way I'm in control. That's what's really important. To be in charge. My anger is what keeps me going. Without it I've got nothing.*

She raised her gun, sighted along it toward the window, saw a movement, and squeezed the trigger. The white handkerchief fluttered to the ground like a fallen bird.

*Good shot!* Crystal smiled a hard, tight smile. *That'll show her.* And she found herself wishing the other five were there to watch and applaud her performance.

But they weren't. Holly and Julia, Meg and Brenda were all back there in the real but infinitely distant world of Abbotsville. As for Sabrina, well, she was probably still sitting under an imaginary rhodo bush in an imaginary park, waiting for the world to become normal again. *Boring*, she told herself. *This place is a lot more challenging. Me against my enemy. Not just Andrea, but everyone who's ever tried to claim me, to control me, all of them stretching back to the distant past, the past I can never quite forget, though the anger helps.*

The street was silent. The wind dropped, so that the tumbleweeds lay like small dead animals along the dusty road.

"Andrea!" she screamed. "Are you still up there? Are you watching me? Come out and show yourself if you dare!"

Silence. *Maybe I have killed her. Maybe she's dead and now I'm really alone.*

"Andrea, answer me! Are you there?"

Silence.

Alone.

Crystal tried to push the idea out of her head, but it came back, like an echo. Alone . . . alone.

"I don't care," she yelled. "Being alone—that's good. No one to bug me any more!" Then she gasped. The false-fronted wooden buildings were fading into mist. The saloon, with its railed porch, seemed to dissolve. The dusty road, the tumbleweeds, all were vanishing.

"No!" she yelled again. "Come back. I made this world. It's mine. I'm in charge. I am!"

She could feel despair dragging her down. It had always been this way: being in charge, then having it taken away from her.

"I made this world. It's mine. I don't care if I'm alone in it. I don't need other people!"

She raised her gun and fired randomly at the fading buildings, at the hard blue sky.

A despairing voice inside her said, *So where is Andrea? Is she dead? Then I really am alone.*

# TWELVE

# ANDREA

How could she explain to anyone that Crystal was lost in some never-ending labyrinth, while Sabrina meditated peacefully beneath a virtual rhodo in a place where time did not exist?

*Sabrina.* "Peace," she had said. Andrea took a deep breath and gathered her scattered thoughts. *I will get through this day,* she told herself determinedly. *Then tonight I will find Crystal.*

She showered, raced to cook Father's breakfast, and hurried to school, imagining that maybe the last three days had never happened, that she would arrive to find everything back to normal, that it had all been a bad dream. Another horrible day at Abbotsville High with the Six still on her case—would that really be an improvement?

She almost bumped into Holly at the lockers and automatically backed off. Then she realized that Holly was backing away from *her* with real fear in her eyes.

She grabbed hold of the strength she got from Sabrina and forced herself to smile. "It's okay,

Holly, honest. I didn't have anything to do with it. I mean . . ." She picked her words carefully. "I mean whatever happened to Crystal and Sabrina was all their doing, not mine."

Holly came close again. "But they *did* vanish," she whispered. "If you didn't make it happen, who did?"

Andrea shrugged. "Like I said, I guess they did."

"I don't believe you!" For an instant Andrea saw anger flare in Holly's eyes. Then it faded to bewilderment. "I sure miss Crystal. I wish she'd come back."

Andrea managed a weak smile. "So do I!"

"You? You're joking."

"Oh, no. I wish . . . I wish that none of this had happened."

The bell went. Andrea slammed her locker and walked down the hall to her first class.

By lunchtime her resolution had faded. Whispered conversations died away as she approached. "Mind if I sit here?" she asked in the cafeteria.

There was an awkward silence. A nudge. Then someone muttered, "Sure. I guess so."

She unwrapped a sandwich. Even with a glass of milk it was hard to swallow, and it left a lump, like a stone, in her chest. The group she was sitting with began talking again, bright artificial exclamations and laughs. Unreal.

It was like that after lunch too—less real than the maze world. She couldn't wait to get away, but the clock moved infinitely slowly.

Her last class was a spare. Thankfully she gathered up her books. *Just let me out of here*, she thought. Then she hesitated. Should I go straight home? Or maybe visit Sofia again? But what was the point? Just to cry on her shoulder and hope to be comforted? *Sofia will be bracing and tell me to get on with it, tell me that it's my maze and that I must make the worlds do my bidding and not Crystal's.* "You do have the courage inside you. You can do it," she had said. No, Sofia would be no help at all.

So she went straight home and cooked an elaborate and tasty dinner, but Father didn't notice, not really. "Thank you, Andrea," he said and opened the book he'd brought from the living room. Andrea sighed. *If only you were the kind of person I could talk to and share things with. How different everything would be.*

Once the dishes were out of the way she locked her bedroom door and took out the maze. Assignments could wait. It was Friday evening and she had the whole weekend in which to do them. Better to get *this* over with.

She looked down at the silver pathway that wound around the black rectangle. *Where is Crystal now?* she thought. *Suppose the dinosaur has eaten her?* Andrea shuddered and told herself not to be stupid. *The maze world isn't real, not in that sense, is it? A person couldn't really get hurt. It is a simulacrum of the real world, Sofia had said. Or is it real?* It was all horribly confusing. And scary.

*Why me?* She found herself wondering. *How come the maze picked me? Or did I pick it?* She tried to get rid of these jumbled thoughts and concentrate on Crystal. "Where are you?" she whispered. And then, to the maze, she said, "Take me to Crystal."

Giddiness. The nauseating sense of being turned inside out. Then the world about her steadied. She blinked and stared around. It made no sense. There was noise. Flashes of light. Like a monumental fireworks display. Mud everywhere. Passages winding here and there, like the maze but dug out of the mud. Duckboards under her feet. She looked down and saw them squishing into the mud beneath her. Then the fireworks display resolved itself into explosives bursting, and debris spattered with dull *whumps* around her. *War! I'm in the middle of a war!* she thought.

She wiped the mud from her face and saw Crystal beyond a tangle of barbed wire, her arms cradling a Kalashnikov. A spurt of bullets whined by like a swarm of angry bees and Andrea ducked, her heart thumping. *Where has Crystal brought me now?*

"Are you there, Andrea? I'm waiting for you." It was like those kids' games: *Come out, come out, wherever you are.*

Andrea took a deep breath and forced herself to move closer, to say calmly, "I'm right here." *But what can I do against this?*

Crystal's furious and destructive images were far

more powerful than anything Andrea could invent. She felt panic rising inside her, and the ferocity of the bombardment seemed to intensify.

"Where are you? Come out where I can see you." Bullets whined by and Andrea ducked again.

"I've killed you, insect, haven't I?"

Inside her head she heard Sabrina's placid voice. "You've got to change Crystal's images into something less harmful." *Flares, not shells*, Andrea thought. *And flowers, not blood*. With a huge effort of will she turned the exploding shells into flares, slowly descending from the black sky, shedding a clear white light on the murky scene below. Then she fashioned the blood into crimson flowers and made them bloom along the mud of the trenches. She could see it happen.

"That's not blood. Look again, Crystal."

She heard Crystal scream. "No! It's not supposed to happen this way! Stop changing things."

"I must," Andrea whispered and took a deep breath. "Put the gun down."

She'd done all that she could do and now she felt that whatever small power she possessed had been drained from her; she was as empty as a dried-up chrysalis. Crystal still confronted her, the Kalashnikov cradled in her arms.

*I can't go on*, she told herself. *Please let it stop*.

She was totally in awe of the power of Crystal, who seemed able to move recklessly from scenario to scenario in the endless possibilities of the maze. Or were they endless? Would there come a time when the maze itself would run out of energy and become a simple, grey-walled labyrinth again? And what would happen to Crystal and Andrea then? Or perhaps Crystal might finally be backed into a corner with no way out, and then—and only then—she might allow Andrea to reach out and help her. Maybe. She hoped so, but obviously not yet.

回

The scenario changed. Andrea was leaning against something, no longer the muddy wall of a trench, but something more solid, almost comforting. There was a hot breeze on her face, and she felt quiet and peaceful.

She looked around and found that she was kneeling on a carpet in an old-fashioned bedroom. The patterns of the carpet and on the wallpaper were blurred, and the four-poster bed was indistinct, as if whoever made this place hadn't bothered with the details. But the window where Andrea was kneeling was clearly defined and the sill felt solid under her elbows. The lace curtain blowing back into her face was almost frighteningly real. She pulled it aside and looked down at the street below. Her eyes watered in the sun's glare on the white dusty road. She blinked and rubbed her eyes. The scene was oddly familiar, as if she'd been here before.

Two rows of wooden buildings flanked the single street. Some had shadowy porches and hitching posts for horses. A sign proclaiming THE OK SALOON creaked in the wind, and a tumbleweed rolled slowly down the street. Andrea almost laughed. This was a place she recognized. It was obviously Crystal's mental reconstruction of a frontier town in the Old West, derived from some old film, like *Tombstone*, or the town in Gary Cooper's *High Noon*.

She leaned out the window and saw Crystal standing, legs astride, in the middle of the road below her. A belt was slung around her waist, guns in the holsters at each hip. She was standing very still and alert, her elbows slightly bent, her fingers open and curved in the stance of a gunslinger sworn to purge the town of its enemies . . . one enemy—Andrea herself.

She bit her lip and drew quietly back from the window. What was she to do? She could think of no way of pulling Crystal back into the real world. To confront her on Main Street would be to play out Crystal's dream of anger and destruction. She was like a bulldozer blundering destructively from world to imaginary world, with only one thought in her mind—revenge. She crouched beneath the window sill and waited, hearing Crystal's challenge. "Come on, Andrea. Where are you? Come out, you coward. Show yourself!"

Should she fight? It would feed Crystal's anger and give her even more power than she already had. No way! There must be something more constructive she could do. Frustrated, she dug her hands into her skirt pockets. Her fingers touched her mother's handkerchief. Was there any magic in it? Handkerchief as in "white flag" was all she could think of. Sabrina's parting word echoed in her head. "Peace!" *Yes, that was it. Not surrender, but a truce. Then see if we can talk things out. If I could just make her understand that I'm not her enemy.*

Would Crystal read the signal that way? No harm in trying.

She pulled the handkerchief from her pocket. It still carried the scent of the fragrance her mother always wore—something with lilies-of-the-valley in it—a scent that brought back mixed emotions. Comfort and well-being on the one hand. Anger and sorrow on the other.

*Mom, why did you have to leave us? Without a word. Not a phone call. Not a letter. Just silence.*

Anger won and hardened and, as it did, she felt the outline of the window sill against which she leaned grow even more solid. Below her she could see the street shimmer more brightly. The wind blew strongly and tumbleweeds rolled between the buildings.

*No. Not anger.* That was the wrong way to go. Sofia had warned her when she gave her the maze, and Sabrina had made it even more clear. She forced her anger toward Mom out of the way and concentrated instead on the message she wanted to send to Crystal. Not surrender—she couldn't give in to Crystal's fantasy—but a truce in which to remind Crystal of the right and orderly world in which people helped instead of trying to destroy each other. She waved the white handkerchief out the window.

"Listen to me, Crystal."

She heard Crystal scream. "That's not my memory! It's yours. I don't want any part of it. You've got no right interfering in my world."

"My world too, now. I got you into this mess," Andrea called down, "though I didn't mean to. So it's up to me to get you out, but you've got to help me. I can't do it alone."

For a moment she thought she had won Crystal over, that the two of them would be able to find their way back to the true maze. Then together they'd find their way to the centre, to the stone at the centre. That's where Sofia said she should go. Crystal had more courage and determination than she had. *Together we can do it*, Andrea realized. But then what? Beyond that moment she had no idea of what might happen. She would have to take it on faith and somehow convey that faith to Crystal.

A shot echoed loudly. Andrea felt a burning pain in her fingers. The handkerchief slipped from her hand to the dusty street below. *Mother's handkerchief!* She ducked back into the shadows and stared in disbelief at her fingertips, mashed and bloody. There was blood dripping down her wrist. Then she felt consciousness slip from her even while she thought desperately: *This is not real. None of this is happening.*

# THIRTEEN

# CRYSTAL

*So where is Andrea? Is she dead? Then I really am alone.*

"Andrea!" Crystal screamed, staring up at the window of the saloon. It was no longer there. Her hand was empty, pointing meaninglessly up at the hard blue sky. The sky, at least, had not changed. The sun still blazed down mercilessly, but nothing else was the same. In front of her, wind-sculpted sand dunes rolled toward a distant horizon.

She spun around. Behind her was more sand, shaped into waves. An ocean of sand with no water in sight. There were no footprints other than her own. There was not a bird in the sky. She was totally alone in a silence so profound that her heartbeat was like a drum.

*I didn't make this world*, she thought and screamed at the emptiness. "Get me out of here!" she yelled. The silence swallowed her words. There wasn't even an echo.

Her knees gave way and she crumpled to the scorching sand, her hands over her face. *Almost like I'm praying*, she thought and rejected the idea.

*I won't let this happen to me!* She forced herself upright again. No one would ever see her grovel. Even in an empty world she wouldn't. She told herself that she'd made the other worlds happen, just with the power of her mind. She, Crystal, had done it. She had shaped the maze with knives and flames, the prehistoric world of primitive emotions, trench warfare, *High Noon.*

Only she hadn't made this desert, had she? Maybe it was a trick of her enemy, Andrea. A trap, that was it. *But does Andrea have the power? Up till now she's been following me. Can she lead? Has she brought me here?*

A chilling thought occurred to her. *Maybe this place is a reflection of what's inside me. Emptiness? Dryness?*

*No!* She pushed the idea aside and tried to plan— to be in charge once more.

"Oasis," she said aloud. "That's what I need right now. An oasis."

She searched her memory. Water, of course, bubbling up from some spring. Even thinking about water tightened her throat. She tried to swallow, licked her dry lips, and forced her imagination to build the place she needed. There would be greenery, of course. And date palms with fresh, sweet fruit. "I *can* do it!" She closed her eyes and willed it to happen.

She took a deep breath and opened her eyes. Nothing had changed. The sun beat down on her head and the ground shimmered in the heat. For the first time in more years than she could remember, Crystal began to cry. The painful tears fell to the hot sand and vanished into the dryness.

*Stop it!* She told herself fiercely. *I can't afford tears. Tears are water and every drop is precious.* She scrubbed her cheeks savagely with her hands. *Somewhere out there in that sea of sand is an oasis. Maybe I don't have to invent it, because it's already there. I only have to find it.*

She stared into the sun-blasted landscape. Was that a shimmer of water over to the right? Small, insignificant, like a fallen contact lens, an oval shimmer just below the horizon. She began to plod through the sand, hope rising inside her. Surely it was a lake? She licked her cracked lips and quickened her pace. It was closer now. She could see it stretching from left to right in front of her. Was she imagining it or could she already see palm trees, a place of shade? She stumbled forward, down the dip of a dune and up another slope. The glimmer vanished, reappeared and vanished again, closing up to a pinpoint and shrinking to nothing.

A *mirage*. That's all it was. Like the patches of wetness on a hot day back home, the blacktop shimmering with water that vanished as one drove closer. Crystal looked back. Her footsteps were a dotted line fading into the distance behind her. She seemed to have come a long way. No point in turning back.

This direction was as good as any. Head down, shoulders slumped, she plodded grimly on.

*This place isn't real*, she told herself. *So how did I get here?* Wearily she thought back to the Wild West, the trench warfare, the dinosaur world, the McGraths. Back into a childhood where memory refused to go. Knives and angry fire instead. Beyond them a grey tunnel. Was the tunnel the end? Or the beginning? No, there was more, wasn't there? The park. The rhodos and that insect Andrea. And a small black box that she and Sabrina had fought over. Yes, the black box was the beginning.

The sun beat down on her head and shoulders. Her eyes ached and the skin of her face felt so tight it might split. She stopped, struggled out of her T-shirt, draped it over her head, and plodded on.

Her eyes were hot stones, burning in their sockets. She couldn't see. She staggered, stumbled, and fell. Her hands were full of sand. Somehow she found the strength to get to her feet once more. She stood for a minute, the sun beating down on her head, felt the world spin around her, and again fell to her knees.

*I'm not going to die out here, am I?*

She must look like the cartoon of a desert explorer, she thought, struggling onward on hands and knees. She found herself smiling at the trite image, and her lips split and stung. She licked them with a tongue swollen and clumsy. For the image to be accurate, the sky above should be full of circling vultures, waiting till she finally fell and lay still.

"Well, I won't give you the satisfaction," she whispered drily and dragged herself on.

Another shimmer tempted her. Was this another mirage? Or the real thing? She imagined she could smell water. She dragged herself painfully forward.

*I won't give in. I never have. That's good, Crystal. Keep going.*

She suddenly realized that there was no anger in this desert world. It was savage enough to kill her, but there was no anger. That had been left behind in the other worlds.

What was that she remembered? A white handkerchief fluttering from a window. *Peace?* Maybe . . .

# FOURTEEN

# ANDREA

*This is not real*, Andrea protested, looking in horror at her mangled fingers. Her head spun. "Not real!" she said aloud and her voice echoed in a different space. She blinked and looked around. The shabby hotel bedroom, the window with the grimy lace curtain, and the sun-blinded street beyond had all disappeared. She was lying on the floor of her comfortingly familiar bedroom. Outside would be streetlights. The park. The world going on in its ordinary way.

*Ouch!* She looked down. Pins and needles prickled through the hand that was doubled under her. She pulled it out, shook it free of cramps, and spread out the fingers, afraid of what she might see. Then she laughed in relief. Five perfectly ordinary fingers, quite intact. She wiggled them.

Of course it hadn't really happened. Mom's precious handkerchief, which had fallen from the saloon window to the dusty street below, must still be tucked in her pocket. She fumbled for it and her fingers closed on a small, hard cylinder, like a bullet.

Her fingers automatically shrank from it. She forced herself to pull out the object. Not a bullet after all. Of course not. Not in this world. Only in the world of the maze. Just her old pink lipstick and, under it, the softness of Mom's handkerchief. She pulled it out and held it to her nose. Was the faint scent real or in her imagination, her memory?

She clutched the handkerchief tightly and tried to reach out to her mother. *Mom, where are you? How could you leave me?* She felt anger stir and quickly suppressed it.

Of course there was no answer. If she wanted one, she would have to look for it herself. *And why not?* she thought suddenly. *I don't have to be as submissive as a pawn in a chess game, just because Father's in charge. I've done the cooking and cleaning, picked up his dry cleaning, and I've never challenged him, not once, nor asked where Mom was and why she hadn't written. Why?*

Fear, she realized. Fear of Father's cold and distant anger—a bit like a freezer burn, which was worse than a scorching rage. *I could have managed better if he'd shouted at me. He sold the house and moved across town and I hardly said a word. I've become his housekeeper. I hate the new school and he doesn't seem to care. He doesn't even listen.*

*Why am I such a coward?* She asked herself. *Where did it begin?*

She could remember everything about that fateful

day, as if it had only happened that morning. The cold, flat taste of soggy cereal, the rain pouring down outside the window, the dining room so dark that the light was on even though it was eight in the morning.

"Where's Mom?"

"She's left us."

"What?" It couldn't be true. She'd heard Mom threaten to leave, but she didn't believe it. She remembered every word.

"You're just teasing, aren't you, Mom? You don't mean it?" she'd begged.

Mom had shaken her head. "I think I'll die or go crazy if I stay here any longer."

But Andrea hadn't believed her—grown-ups didn't talk like that—but by next morning she was gone. She must have packed and left during the night while Andrea was asleep. Not stopping to say goodbye. *Not fair. No! No! No!*

"*Left* us? You mean she's not coming back? You do mean that, don't you, Father? Not coming back ever?" It wasn't real, it couldn't be.

"Exactly. There's a letter for you." He pushed it across the table, touching it only with his fingertips, as if it were soiled. Andrea stared at the single sheet, the words refusing at first to come together and make sense. "I'm sorry" and "I love you. I'll always love you" floated up from the page.

"But I don't understand. Why's she doing this?" she found herself asking accusingly.

*I think I'll die or go crazy if I stay here any longer.* Those had been Mom's words.

Father shrugged. His face was like a stone. "It was entirely her decision, Andrea, not mine."

"But you didn't persuade her to stay? Did you even try?" She stared at his lean face, at the deep-set eyes, struggling to understand. He wasn't a *loving* man, she'd known that for a long time. Not like her friends' dads. But for Mom to leave him . . . to leave *her*. It was unthinkable.

"But—"

"That's enough!" There was a sudden flash of anger in his eyes before his face became stony again.

"Please, what's going to happen to me? When do I get to stay with her? Maybe weekends," she had suggested, remembering her former classmates Marianne and Kathy, whose parents were divorced, so they got to spend alternate weekends with each parent, being spoiled rotten, as they'd gleefully admitted.

Father had shaken his head and his narrow lips tightened. "I am to bring you up and pay for your education. That is the arrangement. There will be no visits."

"You can't stop me from seeing her. I'm going to write and she'll write back. We'll arrange something. You'll see," she shot back.

It was her first and only act of defiance. The coldness between them grew till it was like a wall of ice behind which she shrivelled. She sighed now, remembering, feeling the familiar emptiness inside her.

*If only I'd been more sure of myself,* Andrea thought now. *If I'd just asserted myself. Children have rights too, don't they? I had the right to hear Mom's side of the story—why she left, why she hadn't tried to take me with her. So many "whys."*

Instead she tried to melt the ice, tried to be the perfect daughter, not complaining when he refused to buy new jeans when she outgrew her old ones, or when he refused to allow her to have her hair cut. "You'll dress like a lady and behave like one," he told her.

She begged him not to sell their lovely house and leave the old familiar neighbourhood, but at the end of the school year he bought this cold, impersonal condo in a new neighbourhood. Without a word to her, he cut the final threads that connected her to her memories. A new school, a new neighbourhood. Friendless, she was pitched into the alien world of Abbotsford High. And the Six.

*I can't go on like this,* she scolded herself. *I've got to stop being a coward.* She remembered the trench warfare, the dusty road, and Crystal's guns. *I was brave enough then.*

*Yes, but it wasn't real, was it?*

*Maybe not, but it felt real at the time. I was strong,* she insisted.

She looked at her hand, still clutching her

mother's handkerchief, and remembered the pain and the horror of her mangled fingers. *It's time I stopped being needy and began to act for myself*, she told herself firmly. *I want to see Mom again, and since Father won't help me, I'm going to do it myself.*

*How? No address. No phone number. Where am I to begin?* But Father must have been in touch with her, even if it were only through lawyers. Mom took nothing with her but a few clothes. The rest of her stuff Father had packed in cartons and sent to the Salvation Army. Andrea could still remember the day she came back from school to find empty drawers and a closet of jangling wire hangers.

She got to her feet just as he knocked at her door.

"Time for bed, Andrea."

"Yes, Father. Good night."

He grunted a reply and shuffled off down the passage. She sat on the edge of her bed again and waited until she was sure he was asleep. Then, without giving herself time to have second thoughts, she opened her bedroom door and crept down the dark passage to Father's study. She knew exactly what her goal was—the locked drawer in Father's desk. If there was anything to be found, it would be there. And the lock was no problem, since Father—surely the most precise man on Earth—always left his key ring in the pewter dish in the hall every time he came into the house.

She picked up the collection of keys carefully so

they wouldn't jingle and tiptoed into the study. It took only a moment to find the right key and to slide open the drawer. It was, of course, very neatly arranged, with receipted bills and blocks of old cheque stubs on the left. On the right were packages of letters, tidily filed in their envelopes. Andrea began to riffle through these, her heart sinking as she saw that every one of them was addressed to Father's office—just business stuff then. She had hoped . . . she had been so sure . . .

Then she realized that the top envelope on one small pile was in Mom's handwriting. Of course, Mom didn't know where they lived now. Father wouldn't have told her, which was typical. She could only write to the office. Andrea grabbed it and held it close to her chest, as if the essence of it might some- how be transmitted through the paper to her. It was a temptation to open it and peek at the letter inside, but she resisted it and instead copied down the return address, closed and locked the drawer, returned the keys to their usual place on the hall table, and tiptoed back to her room.

Once safely inside she sat on the bed, hugging the precious piece of paper to her chest. She'd done it! And it hadn't even been difficult. How stupid she had been not even to have tried to trace Mom's whereabouts before. That's what fear did to one. But the influence of the maze seemed to have given her the courage to make a plan and the imagination to carry it out. It was as clear to her as what she had had to do when she got tangled in Crystal's scenarios. Now she had an address and all she needed was the matching phone number. She checked the phone book, but came up with nothing. With her newfound sense of purpose, she dialled 411 and asked for the number of a new listing at the address she read over the phone.

"Name?" the operator asked.

"Rosemary Austin."

Pause. "Nobody of that name at that address."

Andrea hesitated. What had been her mother's maiden name? "Or maybe Rosemary McKay?"

"I do have a listing for a Rosemary McKay," the operator admitted.

Bingo! Andrea fumbled for a pen and scribbled it down.

So far, so good. She looked at her bedroom clock. 10:50. Was it too late to call now? Father always went to bed promptly at ten, but lots of people stayed up much later than that, and if she waited till morning, her sudden courage might evaporate. Quickly she dialled the number and waited, her heart beating hard.

The phone was picked up on the fourth ring, just as she was about to give up.

"Hello?"

She swallowed. "Mom, is that really you?"

Silence. It probably didn't last for longer than a

couple of seconds, but to Andrea it seemed forever. Suppose Mom didn't want to talk to her? Suppose . . . after all, she'd never written to her own daughter in all this time . . .

"Andrea! Oh, my darling girl, where are you?"

"At home. Father's condo."

"I can't believe it. It's been so long since I've heard your voice." Was Mom actually crying? "Why didn't you call me before?"

"I didn't have your number, and I knew Father wouldn't give it to me. Mom, why didn't you write? I waited and waited—"

"But I did. Of course I did." There was a pause. Then Mom's voice hardened. "You never got my letters?"

"Not one. So you *did* write?"

"Again and again. Oh, my dear, you must have thought I'd abandoned you. But it wasn't like that, truly. Your father was supposed to explain, to allow me to write—"

"It's okay, Mom. I've found you. And I want to *see* you."

"And I want to see you. But will your father . . . ? No, of course he won't. We'll have to work this out on our own. Let me think . . . Tomorrow's Saturday. Can you get away? Without a fuss, I mean. We could have lunch out, a whole day together. Can you do that?"

"Oh, yes, Mom. I'll get away. I'll tell him . . . I'll

say I've got to do some research at the library. So where and when will we get together?"

"Wherever you say."

Andrea's brain worked quickly, the courage that she had found in the maze helping her again, putting the words into her mouth. *Unreal!* "The library's open at nine. I'll be there, doing social studies research. No deception."

"I'll meet you there, 9:30 on the dot."

"I love you, Mom."

"Me too times twenty."

It was a very old joke. Andrea felt herself blinking back tears. There, it was done. She was actually breaking out of the prison her father had built around her, and it hadn't been in the least difficult once she found the courage to do it. She picked up the black and silver rectangle from her bedside table. *The maze helped me*, she told herself and began to dream what this first meeting with Mom might be like.

Then reality intervened and she remembered that she and Father always did the week's grocery shopping on Saturday mornings. It was their "family time," she with a grocery list and the cart and he reading labels and putting things he disapproved of back on the shelves. *I'll just slip out and face the music later*, she thought. *He'll flip when he finds out, but I don't care*. She caressed the black oblong with her fingertips. "Thank you for helping me. I know it'll work out."

As soon as the library was open on Saturday morning, Andrea went into the reading room, pulled a book on Canadian history from the shelf, and sat staring at the pages. Now and then she looked anxiously toward the door. The text seemed to dance in front of her eyes . . . 9:20. She tried to concentrate . . . 9:26. She had managed to slip out of the condo without disturbing Father. She'd left a note on the dining table: *Gone to library. Back later*. He'd have to get his own breakfast. *He'll be livid, but I don't care* . . . 9:31 . . .

She took a deep breath, trying to calm her nerves, looked up, and there was Mom. In a moment of panic Andrea had thought she might not recognize her, but of course she did. Mom hadn't changed a bit. They hugged. They stood back and looked at each other. *But she has changed*, Andrea realized. *Nicer clothes, a smart haircut, but more than that*. With a pang Andrea saw that Mom looked *happy*, that the Mom she remembered had never glowed the way she glowed now.

"Let's get out of here," Mom whispered. "There's an espresso bar just around the corner." Once settled down at one of the small tables by the window, they smiled at each other. Andrea's smile was more of a huge grin from ear to ear, she realized. There was a silence and then they both began to speak at once.

"Go ahead, Andrea."

"I've got the whole day. I left a note saying I'd be at the library. I didn't say a thing about when I'd be back."

"Perfect. I've got a plan, if you approve." Then Mom said the words Andrea had dreamed of every time she looked in a mirror, the dream she had shared with the maze. "Would you like to choose some decent clothes and maybe get your hair done while we've got the opportunity? What do you think?"

Andrea drew a deep breath and tried to stop floating up to the ceiling of the coffee bar. "Oh, wow!" She scissored her straight, straggly hair with her fingers. "Mom, could I have my hair cut like this? Just below my ears. And, oh, Mom, can you possibly afford designer jeans and some pretty tops? Father says that clothing a teenager is impossibly expensive and impractical. He says that dresses like this are modest and suitable. But I can't *bear* being modest and suitable and . . . and weird, not any more."

"Nothing's impossible—and you bet I can afford to buy clothes for my own daughter!" Mom laughed. "At first I had a tough time on my own, that's the truth, but I forced myself to buckle down and update my training. It wasn't too hard with no one to criticize me and say I couldn't do it. Then I got lucky and found myself a job with a salary that's more than I need just for myself, so let's go!"

The rest of the morning passed like a dream. The

shopping was done, her hair was shampooed and skilfully cut. They had lunch in a glamorous restaurant where she didn't feel in the least out of place with her new hair and clothes, and where she was allowed to order exactly what she wanted. She felt as if she were walking on air. *It must be my new light haircut*, she told herself. After she said goodbye to Mom, she dropped the shopping bag with her blouse and flowered skirt and the old-fashioned sandals into the Sally Ann bin outside the park. Saying goodbye to her old clothes was a triumph and lessened the sadness of having to say goodbye to Mom.

"You've got my home number and my office number. Work it out with your father and we'll meet whenever you can."

Back at the apartment Father was waiting, at his coldest and most biting. She could feel herself shrivelling, the way a flower must feel after a late frost. She took a deep breath and forced a smile. "Sorry I was gone for so long, but there's still time to shop before the supermarket closes," she forced herself to say cheerfully. "Or we could go tomorrow," she added cunningly.

"On *Sunday*?" He was outraged and began a dissertation on the Lord's Day, but stopped suddenly and stared. "What have you done to your hair?"

"Had it cut. It's neat, isn't it? And easy to look after. Shall we go?"

"And you're wearing jeans . . ."

"We'll have to hurry if we're to get there before the store closes." She swept him out of the house, amazed at her own courage. Even when Father accused her of taking his money to pay for her clothes, she didn't lose her cool. "Count your change," she challenged him. "You won't find a cent missing."

He punished her for her bravado with a cold indifference that was harder to take than a blazing row. She began to understand exactly *why* Mom felt she had to leave. She tried to ignore his icy glare, the few cutting remarks he uttered over that weekend. On Sunday, after church, she vacuumed the apartment, dusted and polished, baked a pie for dessert, and finished the assignments she had skipped on Saturday. No time now for the maze and Crystal, she thought, as she fell into bed with just a small pang of guilt.

Father was still in his icy mood on Monday morning, so it was a relief to escape to school. Then, suddenly nervous about her new appearance, she slipped into a washroom and looked at herself in the mirror. *Mom paid because I didn't have any money, and I took her advice on which clothes looked best and which salon to go to. But it was I, Andrea Austin, who found Mom. Or was it the maze, pushing me to make things happen?*

She peered into the mirror, ran her fingers through her short, wavy hair. The hairdresser had explained how cutting it had released the natural waves. She smiled at her reflection. "I deserve me," she told herself, and then blushed furiously as a group of grade tens came into the empty washroom.

"Hey, cool hair!"

"It that really Andrea? Wow!"

On this wave of approval she was swept out of the washroom and into class. But the sight of Holly and Julia, Meg and Brenda, brought her up short. *Here I am, thinking frivolously about hair and clothes—and there is Crystal, trapped in her angry maze world, and Sabrina. I know Sabrina's okay, but her parents must be worried to death.*

"Did you see it on the news this morning?" someone whispered. "Their pictures and descriptions. Anyone knowing their whereabouts—all that stuff."

Even feeling almost brave as she did, Andrea quailed at the thought of yet another interview with the police; she could see their cruiser out in the parking lot. But it seemed that they had given up believing that she was responsible and were concentrating on the other four, who were taken out of class twice to answer more questions.

*If only I could tell them the truth*, she thought. *But nobody'd believe me, not in a million years.*

"It's all your fault, Four-eyes," snapped Holly as they lined up for lunch in the cafeteria.

Andrea tossed her head, feeling the unaccustomed swish of short hair against her cheeks. "Don't care anyway. Mom's going to make an appointment for me to have laser surgery." She swept past with her tray, leaving Holly standing open-mouthed.

"Over here," someone waved, and she timidly joined the group. It was like a new world. She found she could actually answer without getting tongue-tied or stammering when people talked to her. She joined in discussions, kidded over Ms. Brookes's obsession with *Macbeth*. She was being accepted. Just because of a haircut and designer jeans. Were people that superficial? Was she?

For a minute her optimism slipped. Then she told herself firmly, *It's not the clothes. It's the experience in the maze. Battling Crystal's worlds has made me stronger.* She smiled inwardly at the thought that someday she might tell Crystal how much she owed her. How annoyed Crystal would be!

"What's the joke, Andrea?"

"Nothing," she shrugged. "Just a private thought."

How strange it felt to be dreading home more than school, to have actually *enjoyed* her day. She walked briskly across the park, her backpack slung over her shoulders. Now she could walk past the shadowy rhodo bushes without flinching. Nobody was going to jump out at her.

When Father came home he said abruptly, "Your mother called me at the office."

Andrea's heart flipped. "Oh, yes?"

"She said you intend to go on seeing each other."

"Certainly, we do, Father. Weekends, I expect. Maybe the occasional evening. We'll have to work it out."

"You do realize that I have legal custody?"

"Yes, I do. Mom explained, but I'm sure we'll come to some arrangement. And if there's a fuss with lawyers or anything, I can tell them that I received none of the letters she sent me."

Father was silent. Then he muttered, "So long as it doesn't interfere with your schoolwork—or the housework," he added.

"Don't worry, school will be fine." She swallowed her anger and managed to keep her voice steady and confident. "As for housework, I think we'll have to renegotiate that."

He grunted and looked at her clothes. "Your mother's doing, I presume. I knew she'd be a bad influence. So superficial. Why do you suppose I insisted on sole custody?"

"She's not superficial, Father. She's loving and funny. And alive!" Andrea flared up.

He grunted. "I suppose I must expect to see tattoos and body-piercing next." His voice was icy.

Andrea laughed. "Oh, Father, that's so old-fashioned. Nobody does that any more!"

She left him standing speechless in the hall, carried the dishes through from the kitchen into the dining room. "Dinner's ready, Father. Right on time."

It wasn't a cheerful meal, but it wasn't as bad as

Sunday's had been. Father looked more puzzled than angry, and she suddenly felt sorry for him. He lived in a world of his own, one of numbers and concepts. Maybe it wasn't all his fault.

Andrea puzzled over this new sympathy for Father as she loaded the dishwasher and tidied up the kitchen. Then she finished her assignments, trying to keep her mind on track whenever she found herself thinking about the maze and worrying about what Crystal was plotting now.

# FIFTEEN

## ANDREA

Andrea sat on the edge of her bed, cradling the small black box in her hands, and realized, with a feeling in her stomach like an elevator in free fall, that, though a new hairstyle and designer jeans might prop up her ego at school, they were no help to her in the maze. Within those other dimensions, confronting the manifestation of Crystal's anger in her many-layered worlds, she had nothing but her own courage to support her.

*And that sure isn't much,* she told herself grimly, staring at the box. It was a huge temptation to forget the whole thing for just one night. She imagined herself relaxing in a hot bath with some great bath essence, with a radio and a book to read. But that wouldn't happen anyway. That was a fanciful dream. Father would hammer on the door if she lingered. She hadn't any perfumed bath stuff, and Father would have a fit and lecture her about the possibility of electrocution if she dared to take her radio into the bathroom.

Nice dream, though. One day in the future, when this nightmare was behind her, she would treat herself. "And that's a promise, Andrea," she said out loud.

She gripped the black box, concentrated on Crystal, and, with the now familiar sensation of being turned inside out and then reassembled, she was sucked abruptly into the world of the maze—a very different world. There was sand beneath her feet. The sun, blazing in a molten white sky, stunned her like a physical blow. Silence. Not even a breath of air to stir her hair. Emptiness. Not a footprint. Not a grain of sand moved.

*Oh, Crystal, where are you? What have you done now? And where is "here"?*

No matter where she looked, there was nothing to see but gently rolling dunes, like a frozen ocean. She climbed to the top of the nearest dune and had the dizzying sensation of seeming to see halfway round the world. The sun was dead overhead, casting no shadow. There was no indication of east, west, south, or north. Just one empty, blazing *here*. She turned and turned again. *Where is Crystal?*

She tried to sense Crystal's anger. It had always been so clear, marking a path to where she was, but this time there was nothing. *Nothingness.* It was the essence of this world, a denial of everything. She shivered. This was far worse than Crystal's flaming anger. "She must be here somewhere, or the maze wouldn't have brought me here," she said loudly, arguing with the silence.

She slid down the surface of the dune, scattering grains of sand, and sat cross-legged at the bottom to think. She could zigzag to and fro across this desert for a million years and never find her. Maybe it was time to try to introduce her own scenario, to make a place that would draw Crystal to *her*. Could she do it? Had she the power? It wasn't as if she were fighting Crystal's anger. Sabrina had warned her not to attempt that. Crystal's rage was stronger than anything Andrea could produce to combat it. But there was no anger here. Just an empty world. *I made a new me in the real world*, she told herself. *Maybe I can do as much in the maze world.*

As she sat, she discovered that this world wasn't totally empty. She'd been wrong about that. There was something out there, so alien to Crystal that she had not at first recognized it. A wordless loneliness. And sorrow.

Now she knew. What Crystal needed was a shelter, a welcoming place, where no one had welcomed her before. She needed protection from the burning sun. And companionship. *That* would be the most difficult.

Andrea sat with her eyes closed, her hands lightly folded in her lap, and began to construct this perfect place, a place of refuge. *Water* was the first essential. Water that was sweet, cold, bubbling out of the ground. She imagined it flowing across the small valley in front of her, spreading out to make a lake before trickling away between the dunes. She could hear its quiet murmur over the little pebbles that lined the bottom of the valley. *Yes!*

*Shade.* There should be palm trees. Clustered along the shores of the lake, their shade would protect the more delicate bushes and the flowers that grew beneath them. Dates would hang heavily below the fronds of the palms, a rich mahogany colour, fat, tender, and sweet. She could almost taste them. Her mouth watered. *Yes!*

*Coolness.* She conjured a gentle breeze that rustled the palm fronds and carried the scent of flowers to her nostrils. Many birds, the size of finches and every colour of the rainbow, would be busily darting from bush to bush, eating the seeds, sucking nectar from the flowers. She felt the sweet air and rejoiced in the song of the birds. *Yes!*

She had made it: *an oasis*, complete and perfect.

As she sat quietly with her eyes closed and her hands limply in her lap, she heard the stream chatter, the birds sing; she breathed in the perfume of the flowers, and felt the welcome shade cutting the searing heat of the sun. She knew that when she opened her eyes again, her creation would surround her, like a small jewel. It was made. Now all she had to do was wait.

She opened her eyes, saw its beauty, felt its peace. Then she squinted up into the palms, hand shading her eyes, and decided that she was hungry. After all, she had made this place. Why should she not enjoy it

while she waited? One of the trees was tilted at a rak-
ish angle that made climbing seem possible, even
inviting. She slipped off her shoes, rubbed her hands
against her thighs, and began to climb. The bark was
rougher than the ropes in the gym at school, and the
tree was higher. But she made it at last, struggled to
break off a cluster of dates and then realized that she
couldn't carry it down—she needed both hands on
the trunk—and that if she were to drop them, they
would land in the sand. In the end she tossed them
lightly into the shallow water of the stream.

From this height she could see past the curves of
nearby dunes, way into the distance. Was that a
movement, a long way off across the desert? She
couldn't be sure. She climbed down carefully, lifted
the dates from the water, and plucked a large leaf
from a nearby bush to lay the cluster on.

They looked hugely inviting, mahogany red,
dewed with water. She picked a couple and ate them
slowly, meditatively. The rest she would save for
Crystal, a gift to the girl she couldn't hope to have as
a friend. A sign of goodwill, at least.

She drank sweet water from her hand and leaned
back against the slanting trunk of a palm to wait. She
must have fallen asleep, into dreams of a garden and
Mom coming toward her, a memory of that happiness before the good things ended. Then the dream
changed. Mom turned away and when Andrea
called to her, she didn't listen.

She woke, her mouth open, her throat struggling to form the words that would bring Mom back into the family. Sorrow overwhelmed her in a huge wave. Her eyes opened and she saw her beautiful oasis shudder and begin to fade.

*Crystal!* Andrea pushed aside the cobwebs of sleep and began to concentrate on remaking the oasis. *She's so close*, she realized. *This is her sorrow more than mine.*

*It is not a mirage, Crystal. It is real. Come and drink. Come and eat. Rest in the shade. Be welcome.*

Her vision steadied and, looking beyond the date palms, she could see Crystal crawling agonizingly towards the water, hands clawing the sand, knees shuffling through it. At last she collapsed beside the pool. It was painful to watch, but instinctively Andrea knew better than to interfere. Crystal must find this place on her own, make it *her* refuge.

Only when she had collapsed beside the pool did Andrea lean over her, scooping up water for her to drink. She took Mom's handkerchief from her jean pocket, dipped it in the pool, and washed Crystal's face.

After a while Crystal sat up, groaned, then rolled onto her front and drank deeply from the pure running stream. She saw the dates resting succulently on their leaf and ate them, one by one, tossing their pits into the water. She drank again, sighed heavily, and, for the first time, looked at Andrea.

"I thought I was going to die out there."

"I know."

"*You* made this place?"

"Yes. For you. I made it for you."

"I didn't know you were strong enough." There was a grudging respect in Crystal's voice. "What do you mean you made it for *me*? What's in it for you?"

Andrea forced herself to look directly at Crystal, to see what lay behind those cold blue eyes. She could see only emptiness, and that was even more frightening than the anger and spite she had seen in them back in the real world.

"Why?" Crystal persisted.

Andrea reached inside herself for the truth. "At first I just knew I had to grab you and bring you back to the real world. But then—" She hesitated. "I wanted to end all this blundering from one ugly world to another," she said slowly. "I wanted for both of us to find the centre—the stone at the heart of the maze. And then for us . . ." her voice trailed off.

"To be friends forever?" Crystal gave a hard laugh. "In a pig's eye!"

Andrea flushed. "No. I didn't mean that . . . I don't suppose . . . we're so different. Our growing up has been in such different directions, hasn't it? But I thought that maybe we could . . . connect." Her voice faded at the expression on Crystal's face.

Crystal picked up the handkerchief Andrea had used to wash her face. It had already dried in the fierce heat, even under the shade of the palms. She waved it, it seemed to Andrea, in mockery of Andrea's gesture of a truce back in the Wild West.

Andrea bit her lip. "At least I wouldn't try to shoot you in reply," she snapped.

This time Crystal's laugh was genuine. "And I'll never surrender, Andrea. You know that's not my style. But if you do know a way out of here, I'll tag along."

"No surprises? Promise?"

"Meaning exactly what?"

"You know. Flames. Knives. Man-eating dinosaurs . . . all that sort of stuff."

Crystal shook her head. "I'm tired, Andrea. I just want to get out of here."

"I don't know if I can do it if you just tag along. I think I'll need your help."

"Whatever."

"It's all a mind game. You know that, don't you? No, not really *mind*—more like feelings, emotions. We've got to believe in the possibility of change. To image ourselves back to the way the maze was at first. Just a sort of grey plastic passage—a *peaceful passage*. Once we get there, we must find the centre, the stone at the heart of the maze."

"Why?"

Andrea shrugged. "I don't know, but Sofia—she was the one who gave me the maze—told me that."

"And then what's supposed to happen?"

"I honestly don't know, but I trust Sofia. It's more difficult for you, I know. You've never met her. But my life has changed since she gave me the maze—I've changed." She hesitated and then went on, stumbling to find the right words, not to turn Crystal off, not to provoke the anger that must still lie there under the surface. "It's kind of like faith, a reaching out to grab the rope when you're about to fall off the cliff. You don't stop to argue. You just grab it. Does that make sense?"

To her relief, Crystal laughed. It didn't have a lot of humour in it, but it was still a laugh. "Okay. I've fallen off a few cliffs in my time, so I guess I'll go along with you. The alternative's not that attractive. And I'm tired, tired to the bone." She sighed deeply, then sat up, staring at Andrea with some of her old imperiousness. "But don't let it go to your head," she warned.

"And don't you," Andrea dared to retort. "Just follow my lead and I think we'll be okay."

"Think? You're the one holding the rope, Andrea Austin."

Andrea managed a weak smile and concentrated. *Goodbye, oasis. It's hard to let go of shade, coolness, precious water.*

The oasis was gone, and here was Crystal's world of white heat and blazing sun. "Together," Andrea whispered. "Greyness. Quiet. Shadowy passages."

"Boring!" said Crystal. The heat and light shimmered.

"Please," she whispered again. "Help me remake the maze. I can't do it alone."

She closed her eyes and concentrated. Slowly the hot, gritty sand became a floor, smooth and cool.

Cautiously she opened her eyes. *Yes!* They had done it! She scrambled to her feet and held her hand out to Crystal. Reluctantly Crystal grasped it, stood up, and looked around.

"That's what it was like at first, before—"

"Hold onto that thought," Andrea interrupted her. "Nothing else. Don't even think of what it turned into afterwards. Just think 'grey and peaceful.'"

"Okay, boss. Whatever you say. What next?" Crystal's voice was edgy and flippant—hiding her real feelings, Andrea thought, looking at her anxiously. Could Crystal be trusted to keep her anger under control? She realized that her own attitude had changed. At first she'd been terrified of Crystal. If she'd sprouted horns or fang-like teeth, Andrea wouldn't have been surprised. *But now she's different—or maybe I am. Under the facade of the bully I can feel her loneliness.*

*Hold onto that thought*, she told herself and smiled. "Your guess is as good as mine. I've no idea which is right, but I believe that if we *think* we're choosing to find the heart of the maze, that's what we'll find. The stone at the heart of the maze."

Crystal shook her head slowly. "You're weird, d'you know that? But whatever it takes to get us out of here, okay."

"You've got to really believe that's what you want, Crystal. It's no good just going along with me or it won't work. You've really got to want to get back to the real world."

"That's the catch, isn't it? Maybe I'm not that crazy about the real world."

"I know what you mean. But think about it, Crystal. You changed the maze to what you thought you wanted, even though that turned out to be a dead end. Maybe we can change the real world—the bits of it that touch us—or change our attitude."

"Don't you dare preach! You sound like the McGraths."

"McGraths?"

"My grim foster parents," Crystal muttered. "You don't want to know."

"Sorry. I didn't mean to. Well, are you ready for it? Shall we try?"

Crystal shrugged. "I guess so. But do I have to keep holding your hand?"

"I think so. Sorry about that. I guess it's a kind of insurance. I can't stand the thought of having to hunt for you through another zillion universes." She smiled, trying to make a joke of it.

Crystal shrugged again. "Okay, so which way do we go?"

"The way that feels right—for both of us. We have to agree on it or it won't work."

They set off down the grey passage until they came to an intersection. It took a while for them to be sure. Left? Or right? Finally they chose the right-hand path, and next time the left. With each choice it became clearer that only one way would lead them to the centre. It was with a sense of joy—of home-coming—that they walked faster and faster along the labyrinthine paths, no more able to resist the pull than iron filings could resist a magnet.

"This is so right! Crystal, can you feel it?"

"Oh, yes!"

Andrea saw that she was smiling and that her eyes shone. She looked transfigured.

The way ahead became steadily brighter, glowing with a clear gold light. Abruptly the path divided, curving left and right to become a circular space. At the centre of the circle was a pillar, on top of which something shone so brightly that they automatically put up their hands to shield their eyes, as if they were looking at the sun.

Andrea could hear music. Not any instrument that she could name—perhaps the delicate inter-mingling of a hundred violins, a hundred flutes. No, not quite like that either. Maybe it was more like an enormous choir humming a wordless song. Andrea felt a healing sense of peace and rightness. It was as if they had come to the centre of the universe, where there were no more puzzles and everything became clear. She took her hands from her face and stared.

"Do you hear it, Crystal?" she whispered. "Do you *see*?"

Crystal squeezed her hand and they stood silently, bathed in light and music for what seemed like a long time—or maybe it was no time at all.

꠴

Slowly Andrea felt her body melt out of its strange trance. Her brain began to stir with a myriad of questions. *What is it? What are we looking at? What does it mean?*

As her eyes adapted to the brilliant light, she could see *it* more clearly. The stone at the heart of the maze? No, it definitely wasn't a stone. Like a beach ball, close enough to touch? Or huge, unbelievably heavy, and a very long way off?

Suspended in golden light above the central pillar, its colours seemed to change in subtle ways, swirling curves of white and blue.

"What is it, Crystal? What do you think?"

"It reminds me—oh, yes! It's a model of Earth. A living model."

Once Crystal had identified it, it was perfectly obvious. A model of the classic, never-to-be-forgotten view of Earth as seen from the surface of the moon, all those years and years before. A model to be seen in any planetarium. It was breathtakingly beautiful and peaceful, but there seemed to be no purpose that Andrea could discern in its presence here, at the heart of the maze. It simply *was*.

"So what now? Are we just going to stand and stare at it? Come on, Andrea. It's *your* maze. What's supposed to happen next?"

"*Our* maze. Mine to start with, but you took it over and made it yours. And Sabrina made it hers— a very different world."

"Maybe I did, but not like *this* place. This is more yours than mine."

Andrea tried to make sense of it, to put her feeling into words. "It's got something to do with time, hasn't it?" she said at last. "Earth keeps time for us, doesn't it?"

"More the sun and moon, I'd say."

"Yeah, but seen from Earth. Spinning Earth." She stared up at the blue-and-white sphere.

"So?"

"There's a puzzle I still don't understand, something that's built into the maze. I can go in and out, have an adventure, whatever, and no time has passed when I come out, though it feels as if I've been gone for hours. But you and Sabrina are different. You've been trapped in the maze since last Tuesday—six days and nights—and that's real time. You and Sabrina are missing from the real world."

"What do you mean, *last* Tuesday? What day is it now?" Crystal's voice went up.

"It's Monday night. Six days and nights. Time *has* passed for you and Sabrina."

"*Six days!*" Crystal gasped and then recovered. "So what's your point?" she snapped.

"I don't really know, but this is the timekeeper."

"Timekeeper for the maze worlds, you mean."

"Yes. If we're going to get you and Sabrina out of here and restore real time for you, we're going to have to—"

"Stop the clock," Crystal interrupted. "Like 'Stop the world. I want to get off.'"

Before Andrea could stop her, before she could even guess her intention, Crystal reached out both hands to the spinning sphere.

"Don't! Oh, be careful!"

Andrea's warning cry echoed around the maze. There was a lurch, like the sudden braking of a streetcar, like an earthquake. They staggered, lost their balance, and fell. The lights flickered, the music died away. They got to their knees and helped each other to their feet.

"What happened?"

"It did stop! We're here. We're back." Crystal's voice was triumphant. "Look!"

At the end of a quiet grey passage was a glimpse of green grass, of the sun shining in a normal blue sky. Rhodo bushes . . .

"Why, this is where Sabrina went, to sulk under a rhodo bush, I guess," Crystal exclaimed.

"Not to sulk. You'd be surprised. Sabrina made a refuge, not just for herself. She built a world of peace, when the maze was filled with anger. Without her strength, I couldn't have reached you."

"Sabrina? That crybaby?" For an instant Crystal frowned. Then she managed a wry smile. "So I guess the maze changed her."

"As well as us," Andrea reminded her. "And I'm not doing a 'McGrath' on you. We *are* changed."

Sabrina came to meet them, her hands outstretched. "It worked! You've done it! I was watching the sky, thinking of you, and suddenly the clouds began to move again. I could feel the breeze. And there are people walking."

Andrea took her hand and, after a pause, Crystal took the other. Crystal looked at her doubtfully. "You *have* changed."

"For the better, I hope." Sabrina smiled. "A person can't meditate over their whole life without some changes happening."

Andrea saw Crystal flinch and realized that, for her, reliving her life was the last thing she wanted.

"It's okay," she said softly. "The world is going on. Time for us to join in."

The ordinary world was bathed in a golden light. It was beautiful, even the squashed cigarette carton and a dented soft-drink can. In the distance Andrea could see a woman push a baby carriage. Another walker was propelled along by two eager Samoyeds, their white tails waving. A puppy bounded down the path toward them.

"It's okay. Come on! This is exactly as it was last Tuesday, when it all began." Andrea pulled on Crystal's and Sabrina's hands and felt a small explosion, as if they had pushed against a plastic film that suddenly gave way. Evening sunshine lay over the park. There was the scent of newly mown grass.

Yes, time to join in. A new beginning, maybe.

# SIXTEEN

# ANDREA

Home. The same, but not the same. There were the joggers. A mother pushing a pram. A dog . . .

But then the four burst out from behind the rhodo bushes. Crystal pulled her hand away from Andrea's. Her expression was not of anger but bewilderment. Sabrina stretched and looked around her, a smile of pleasure on her face.

"Crystal, what are you doing?" Holly yelled. "We planned—"

"Yeah, let's go," Julia broke in.

Crystal looked at Andrea, a half-smile on her face. "Cool it, girls."

In that frozen instant, as Andrea tensed, waiting for the expected attack, the attack she remembered, for time to rerun itself from last Tuesday, a small blue ball marbled with white rolled slowly before coming to a stop on the path at Crystal's feet. The puppy, a fat white puppy with a comical blot of black over its right eye, waited, tail wagging, round body shivering in anticipation, its tongue, like a strip of pink flannel, lolling from its mouth.

"Reminds me . . ." Crystal stooped, picked up the ball, and stared at it. She smiled. "Well, then . . ." She rolled it between her fingers and tossed it in the air. Andrea watched it spin, white streaks like swirls of cloud. Crystal caught it and threw it in a great arc across the grass. "Go for it, buster!" she yelled. The puppy turned and raced away. Crystal laughed and grabbed Sabrina by the shoulder. "Glad to see you in the real world again."

"And I'm glad to see you, Crystal. A new start?"

"Don't push it," Crystal warned, but her voice was light. She turned to Andrea. "And you'd better be on your way before these puppies of mine make a salad out of you."

*A salad?* Andrea swung her backpack more securely on her shoulder and walked away. Her mind shuttled to and fro as she tried to weave together what had actually happened at this encounter in the park. Happened? Or not happened? She tried to work it out.

To the four in Crystal's gang no time had passed. Last Tuesday afternoon was also this Tuesday. They had waited for Andrea in the park—and let her go. Crystal and Sabrina had never vanished. There had been no police interviews, no days of suspicion and fear. Only she, Crystal, and Sabrina had lived that extra week outside ordinary time, a time that was slowly fading from her memory, like a dream.

As Andrea walked along, the wind blew her skirt,

tangling it in her legs. Skirt? Hadn't she tossed her skirt into a Salvation Army bin, thankful for the freedom of new, well-cut jeans? She stopped abruptly and looked down at her skirt, at her depressing sandals. She became aware of her hair dragging on her shoulders, tangling in the breeze. No visit to Mom, no shopping with her. The *old* Andrea. The Andrea of last Tuesday.

Or this Tuesday? Were they the same?

She knew in her heart that a week *had* gone by, with all its terrors, but bringing also its gift of self-knowledge, of growth. *I don't feel like the old Andrea,* she protested.

She recalled the expression on Crystal's face. *And you'd better be on your way before these puppies of mine make a salad out of you.*

And Sabrina's smile. The peace sign.

She wasn't crazy. *They remembered what had happened in that week carved out of time, that week that wasn't a week at all, but a space in which to remake themselves.*

She walked more slowly as memories flashed across her mind like scenes from a movie, some as clear as if she'd just seen them, others more foggy, blurred by time. Would the rest fade too? Would she eventually lose all memory of this week, as if it had never happened?

Outside the condo block the doorman stood, taking in the sun. "Evening, Miss Austin."

"Good evening." She unlocked the security door, called the elevator, and pushed the button for the eleventh floor. Father wasn't home yet. She was all right. *Well, of course*, she told herself. *I'm home in lots of time. Why wouldn't I be?* The word "time" jangled in her memory.

The apartment was cool and quiet. She put her backpack in her room, put rice on to boil, a couple of chicken legs in a marinade of soy sauce and honey. She turned on the broiler and washed and spin-dried the lettuce. She was just setting the table when she heard his key in the lock. She went into the hall to greet him.

"Hello, Father. Did you have a good day?"

He grunted. "Not particularly. Left my notes on the bus. Can't think how it happened. I'll have to prepare them all over again for next week's lectures."

"Maybe someone will turn them in."

"Not likely. People don't care about other people's belongings nowadays. They'll be just tossed in the garbage, I expect." He sighed heavily and walked toward his room. "I need dinner in five minutes," he turned back to warn her.

"I do remember, Father." She pushed down a sudden surge of anger, remembering some promise she'd made to herself, some sort of resolution. *Peace*, Sabrina had said. Hadn't she? It had been very important, she thought, grasping at the tatters of memory.

As usual they ate in silence. *He's upset because of his*

*lost notes,* she told herself. For once she was glad of the silence. She felt out of sync with the world around her, as if the dining room, her father, the meal they were eating, were not quite real. *Like when I had the flu,* she thought. Finally Father stood up. "I expect to be home by ten."

"Yes, Father."

"Make sure you've done your assignments."

"Of course, Father."

The door shut with a bang. Andrea cleared the table and put the plates and pans in the dishwasher. She settled down to homework.

She was startled by a ring at the door. Nine-thirty. Too early for Father. And surely he would have remembered his key. She went to the door and looked through the peephole. A uniformed cop stood outside. Her heart gave a guilty jump. But what did she have to be guilty about? She slipped on the security chain and opened the door a crack.

"Constable Bruce Cook." He showed her his ID. A face that matched the photograph, and a reassuring smile. She opened the door.

"Come in." She had an odd sense of déjà vu, as if this scene had already been played through. The lost week. This Tuesday or last? A policeman? But the memory had vanished like a soap bubble, like a dream. The policeman was talking to her and she pulled her attention back. "I'm sorry. What did you say?"

He was holding out a sheaf of papers to her.

"These were turned in at the bus depot. This address. They seemed important. Can you identify them?"

She stared blankly and then woke up. It was her father's handwriting. "Why, they're the papers Father left on the bus this afternoon. He will be so glad to have them back. Thank you very much for delivering them in person."

"You're welcome, Miss. I was in the depot on other business and it was on my way."

He left and she stood by the open door, the sheaf of notes clutched to her chest. Just for a moment she had imagined something very different . . . something scary.

She left the papers on the hall table for Father to find when he got home and went to her bedroom. In her closet was a cardboard box full of precious mementoes. She hadn't looked at them since they moved, but now she felt suddenly drawn to the box. She sat on the floor and sorted through the contents, remembering. There was the pale pink lipstick that she had dared to buy and wear—just once—before Father forbade it. And there was the fine cotton handkerchief that had belonged to her mother. She held it to her nose, imagining she could still smell her mother's distinctive perfume.

*I do miss you, Mom. Why did you leave without a word? Why have you never written or phoned? It is as if you were dead, but you can't be, can you?*

She remembered looking up "Rosemary Austin" in the phone book and failing to find a listing. And she had let it go. All this time she had been like one of those patient females in folk tales waiting for someone else to rescue her. She had allowed Father to bully her, to turn her into a servant, to make her wear ridiculous old-fashioned clothes and keep her hair in a totally outdated style, and she'd done nothing about it.

Or had she? *Meeting Mom and having her pick out new clothes for me, choosing a hairstyle. Just a wish-fulfilment dream.* She sighed. *In your dreams, Andrea Austin. It never happened. But it could. I can make it happen if I choose.*

Right now she felt amazingly capable and brave, quite different from her normal meek self. She stared at her reflection in the mirror on the bureau. She *looked* the same. "But I have changed, I know it," she said aloud. *Whatever happened in that vanished week has changed me. I can do it. I can try anything.*

Father wasn't going to be home for another quarter hour or so. She went into his study and quickly checked the desk drawers. The third one was locked. He wouldn't keep the key on his person, she thought. He liked his jacket pockets flat and smooth. It was probably in his room, in the bowl where he kept spare change and cufflinks.

And there it was. She scooped it up, ran back to the study, and unlocked the mysterious drawer. She stared at the paper-clipped piles of paid bills and a stack of cheque stubs, all as tidy as she'd expected. But on the right, stuffed at the back, was a small pile of envelopes, held together with an elastic band. She felt guilty as she reached for them. What would Father do if he could see her now, prying into his private affairs? She pushed the guilt aside—*my affairs too*, she told herself—and forced herself to pick up the package. The envelopes were all addressed to Father at his office address. Her heart sank. Just business stuff. But the handwriting was Mom's, wasn't it? An unfamiliar return address, but in Mom's hand.

She grabbed the pile, closed the drawer, locked it, and had just taken the letters to her bedroom when she heard him come in. There was an exclamation of surprise. "My notes!"

She slipped the package into her skirt pocket and went into the front hall. "Yes, isn't it great? Someone turned them in at the bus depot and they gave them to the police. A constable brought them over in person. Wasn't that kind?"

"Well, wonders will never cease!" For a moment his face relaxed into a half-smile, but then his mouth twisted in that cold smile that Andrea knew and dreaded, almost as if he were disappointed that people hadn't lived *down* to his expectations.

"Good night, Father. I'm so glad it turned out okay." She turned away with the guilty feeling that he might see through her skirt pocket to the package hidden there. When she was safely in her own room, she slipped the elastic band from around the envelopes. They were already in chronological order and she looked at the first, dated shortly after Mom left. She took a deep breath, torn between feeling it was wrong to read someone else's correspondence and the need to know where Mom was and why she had left without a word.

The words blurred and she had to blink and rub her hand over her eyes.

"Please don't blame me so, Matthew. I'd have stayed if I could . . . so cold to me. How have I disappointed you? Or was that iciness always there? No, I can't believe that. I did love you once, until you froze me out, so I must believe that there was once a warm person whom I could love . . . I know you were bitterly disappointed when you were passed over for the appointment you so craved, but we could have overcome that and gone on together, if you had allowed it . . . Year after year you diminished me, until there was almost nothing left of me, or our love. I had to escape . . . I was so unhappy I was afraid. For myself. For Andrea. Please help her to forgive me . . . Let me visit her once I'm on my feet again . . . I love her so. I'd love you if you'd let me, but you've pushed me away."

Andrea clutched the letters to her chest. Mom *did* love her—had always loved her—had wanted to write to her. So what had happened? She quickly scanned the remaining letters. They had all been addressed to Father's office. The message in each of them was almost the same.

"I went past the house today and see there's a 'For Sale' sign up. Please let me know where you're moving to. I still haven't had a word from Andrea in answer to my letters. Does she hate me for leaving her? Is she well? Is everything all right? I tried to phone Andrea, but your new number is unlisted. Matthew, please . . ."

Andrea put the last letter down with a trembling hand. Unkind and ruthless, Mom had called him, and that is why she left. Andrea no longer felt guilty about reading them. "I just wish I'd done it sooner," she muttered to herself as she copied down the return address on the front of the most recent letter. Then she tiptoed into Father's study and returned the letters to the drawer and locked it. She could hear him in the bathroom vigorously brushing his teeth and grabbed the opportunity to slip into his bedroom and return the key to its place.

Back in her bedroom Andrea hesitated. Should she find out her mother's phone number and call her now? She imagined herself arranging to meet her on the weekend. *Didn't I dream of doing that?* Struggling to make up her mind, she stared blankly at her reflection in the mirror. Long, lank hair. A droopy cotton skirt. Yuck!

*I don't want Mom to see me like this. I want Mom to see the new me. Tomorrow's Wednesday,* Andrea reminded herself. *Tomorrow I'll call her, and do everything else I need to do.* She fell asleep planning, and in the morning she knew exactly what she was going to do. It was an outrageous plan. Maybe it wouldn't work. Maybe Crystal would cream her, but it was worth trying. She knew she couldn't do it alone, and she had the weird but strong feeling that Crystal would be the one to help her. For luck she tucked the strange black box Sofia had given her into her backpack.

"I need a considerable amount of money for a project, Father," she said boldly as she served his breakfast.

"A school project?" He looked suspicious. "I can let you have ten dollars." He pulled out his wallet.

"That's not nearly enough, I'm afraid. A hundred might just cover it, one-fifty would be better."

She waited for the explosion, promising herself she wouldn't flinch or back down.

"A hundred and fifty dollars! You must be mad! Do you think I'm made of money?"

"It's actually a bargain, Father. You've never given me a regular allowance, and just think of all the money you've saved by having me act as cook and housekeeper ever since Mom left. I'm sure *she* didn't expect you to skimp on my needs."

With butterflies fluttering in her stomach, she looked him straight in the eye. She saw a spark of anger fade into uncertainty. *Keep calm*, she reminded herself. *Don't let him intimidate you.* His eyes dropped. Amazingly his fingers dipped into his wallet and pulled out three fifties.

"This mustn't get to be a habit," he said predictably. "And I shall expect a full accounting of your expenditures."

"Yes, Father. Thank you." She tucked the money into her skirt pocket, grabbed her backpack, and scurried for the elevator before he could change his mind. Her hands were sweating and she was breathing hard, but she'd done it. She couldn't believe she'd actually done it. Now perhaps the next, even more difficult step would not be too hard.

She had made no real friends at school. There was no one to whom she could turn for advice. Except her enemy. An enemy who felt as close as a friend. *Does Crystal feel the same way? Or will she trample all over me?* It was an outrageously daring idea, but worth the risk.

She strode into school, took a deep breath to quiet the butterflies in her stomach, and boldly headed for Crystal's locker. The other four were clustered around. *But where's Sabrina?* And another memory stirred, reminding her of the new Sabrina, who no longer wanted to be part of the gang.

Andrea wanted to turn and run. She made herself stand firm. "Hi, there," she said, her mouth dry, and managed a smile.

"You talking to me, insect?" A bad beginning, but Andrea felt that the words had come out automatically, that Crystal wasn't really mad at her.

She swallowed. "Yeah. I really need your help. Could I talk to you alone, just for a moment?"

Crystal stared at her silently, but Andrea could see the curiosity in her eyes. She jerked her head toward the other four. "See you guys later." When they were alone she said, "So? Why should I help you?"

"No reason. I just thought you'd be the best one. You see, I'm sort of escaping from my father."

There was a gleam of interest in Crystal's eyes. "What d'you mean, 'sort of'?"

"I want to remake myself, but I know I can't do it alone."

"Why should I care? What's it to me?"

"A dare," Andrea suggested. "Like a challenge. Surprise the heck out of everyone. Are you on?"

"Maybe. What have you got in mind?"

Andrea explained exactly what she wanted to do. ". . . and I've got a hundred and fifty bucks. I don't know. Will that be enough?"

Crystal actually chuckled. "You've got a nerve, I'll say that for you. I didn't think you had it in you. What a surprise! Yeah, it'll be a riot. Let's go for it. Come on." She slammed her locker shut.

"You mean now? Skip class?"

"You got cold feet? Don't wimp out or you can just forget the whole deal."

"Okay. I'm on." Andrea dumped her backpack in her locker and the two of them ran out and caught the next bus downtown.

Once they were in their seats Andrea took a deep breath. "I've got a weird question, Crystal. Okay?"

"Maybe."

"I've changed a lot, and I thought maybe you had too. You and Sabrina. Do you remember why— what happened?"

"Remember?" Crystal blinked, a sudden uncertainty in her expression.

"A Tuesday—and another Tuesday. And the time in between. A time that's there and not there. Whenever I try to grab hold of it, it's gone. Kind of like a dream."

Crystal shook her head as if she were trying to get rid of a fogginess. "I don't know . . . maybe . . . You are weird," she said at last.

"We all three are."

"Speak for yourself," Crystal snapped, but with a smile that took the edge off her words. "A Tuesday and another Tuesday. Maybe. My business what I remember. You're right about Sabrina, though. She *is* different. And that's *her* business, I guess. I'm sorry she doesn't want to be part of the gang any more."

"You might enjoy teaming up with the new Sabrina rather than with Holly and that lot."

"Don't push it or I'll regret saying I'll help you,"

Crystal warned. "Now tell me again what you're planning."

"A haircut and some cool clothes, only not expensive."

"Well, you've picked the right person, I'll say that for you. I can sniff out a bargain better than anyone. Now, listen up. You're in my hands now. No backing off."

*No backing off*, Andrea told herself, though her heart sank as Crystal swept her into a hair salon that was all chrome, black and shiny, a place she would never have dared enter on her own.

"Now this is a really neat place," Crystal told her. "And since it's early, we shouldn't have to worry about an appointment." She pushed Andrea ahead of her, bullied one of the elegant hairdressers, and had Andrea sitting in front of a mirror before she'd had time to protest. *I'm in your hands*, she silently told the hairdresser, whose smooth black hair was cropped into jagged points. The contrast between Andrea's limp locks and her way-out style was too pitiful. Andrea shut her eyes.

But when they left the salon an hour later, it was okay. *Very* okay. Andrea felt light-headed, with a new feathery cut that seemed, by some miracle, to have produced waves in hair that had always been as straight as a ruler. "Not surprising it was so straight," the stylist had told her, "with all that weight pulling it down."

By now the stores were just opening and Crystal dragged her ruthlessly from place to place, in and out of change rooms. "I've only got a hundred dollars left," Andrea warned.

"It's knowing what to look for and where," Crystal told her. "D'you think I'm made of money? No way. Now try this. Okay, that's great! No, don't take it off, stupid! You're not planning to wear that skirt ever again, are you? That's good, because I wouldn't be seen dead with you around school looking the way you did. It would totally destroy my image."

Andrea laughed. "I promise. And hey, Crystal, thanks a million. You've been great. That was quite a challenge."

Crystal grinned. "Yeah, it was that, but worth doing." She looked appraisingly at Andrea. "My handiwork. I could almost be proud of you."

Andrea laughed. "Don't overdo it!" She looked at her watch. "If we hurry we'll be just in time for biology."

"Good grief! You mean you're keeping track of class times? That's really creepy." But Crystal's voice was agreeable, and she hadn't called Andrea "insect" once. "Why not skip the rest of the day? What the heck!"

"Up to you, but I'm dying to go back and make an impression on the class with the new me. Anyway, I *like* biology."

Crystal hesitated. "I don't want to miss everyone's

face when they see the new you for the first time. Okay."

They swept into biology, just as Ms. Williams was handing out specimens. "Crystal, you're late. Take a demerit."

"It's my fault, Ms. Williams. I had an emergency and she was helping me out," Andrea said hastily.

"And you're . . ." Ms. Williams did a double take. "*Andrea Austin?* Class, quiet down. You've seen someone with a haircut before, I presume. Emergency? Well, I'll let you get away with it this time. You two will have to be partners for this lab. Everyone else is already paired up. Now get going and don't waste time."

"Okay with you if we're partners, Crystal?" Andrea whispered.

Crystal shrugged. "Guess so. If you promise not to barf like Sabrina did that time we dissected the pig fetuses."

# SEVENTEEN

# CRYSTAL

*Okay with you if we're partners?* Sometimes a person's words linger long after they are spoken and gone, almost as if the ear has a memory of its own, as if certain important ideas are stored in a closet with a door that refuses to shut completely, that keeps swinging open.

"Okay with you if we're partners?" Andrea's words, meaning exactly that: working on the same specimen, dissecting, drawing, labelling the various parts.

As they worked, Crystal found herself savouring the word. *Partners*. Sometimes it came to her with a Western twang—"pardners." And she had a mental image of a dusty street and tumbleweed.

When the biology lab was over, Andrea vanished on some business of her own, and Crystal found herself drifting over to the library, a place she normally never entered except when forced. A dictionary . . . Obviously there would be one in here, but she was too proud to ask and wandered from shelf to shelf until she discovered it.

Partner: A person who possesses something jointly with
another.

A person who takes part with another in doing
something.

A player on the same side in a game.

With one finger keeping her place in the dictionary, Crystal looked absently round the room. She
had a table to herself. Already her reputation at
Abbotsville High had made sure of that. *No partners
here, pardner.*

A person who possesses something jointly with another.
*Not me,* she thought. *I share nothing with anyone, not
feelings, not memories. Definitely not memories.*

A person who takes part with another in doing something. Her finger hesitated on the line. There was the
biology lab, of course. No big deal. But the shopping
spree, now that was definitely weird. Weird that
Andrea had the nerve to ask. Even more weird that
she'd taken the challenge. Why had she?

Crystal found herself reliving the events and the
odd sensation of pride that swept over her when
Andrea emerged, like the swan in the Disney cartoon, changed from the ugly duckling.

In her mind's eye she could see Andrea's limp
brown hair falling to the floor under the scissors of
the stylist, and the transformation brought about by
the auburn rinse to the shiny waves that remained.
She could see that awful flowered skirt in a ring on

the floor as Andrea stepped out of it into the jeans that showed off her long slim legs, her flat stomach and shapely butt.

*As proud as if I were a mom*, she found herself thinking, and gave herself a mental shake. *I must be going soft in the head. When did I ever know a mom that cared?*

One more definition. A player on the same side in a game. Same side? She wasn't on the same side with anyone, was she? She never had been. *A loner and proud of it*, she thought, and had to blink back unexpected tears. *I must be coming down with flu or something.* That would account for the fuzzy feeling in her head, the feeling that she'd been here before, that she'd lived this Tuesday before—only differently.

*A player in a game.* Yes. *On the same side.* Definitely not. It was maddening. It was as if not one word but a whole story was on the tip of her tongue, ready to be told. And if only she could remember this vanished story, everything would be transformed. If only . . .

*New beginnings.* Maybe they were possible anyway. Sabrina had said something—darn, she'd forgotten what that was too. Her mind was definitely going—early-onset Alzheimer's maybe.

She shook her head as if to get rid of all these disconnected thoughts. *New beginnings.* Maybe she should hang onto *that* thought.

Crystal pushed the dictionary aside and walked quickly out of the library and down to her locker. The four were hanging around waiting for her. Not

Sabrina. That was okay. She figured that she and Sabrina had had some kind of confrontation—not unfriendly, but final.

Crystal found herself wishing that Andrea were still hanging around the lockers too. Maybe she could show off her ugly-duckling-into-swan again. Maybe not a good idea.

*Well, there goes another Tuesday.* She opened her locker.

# EIGHTEEN

# ANDREA

After the biology lab Andrea had a spare, and she pocketed some quarters, grabbed a pay phone, and dialled 411. They'd been no help before, but now, thanks to the letters in Father's desk, she had an address and her mother's maiden name. She was answered by a recording in her mother's familiar voice that gave a work number. Her hand trembling, she punched it in.

"The office of Dwight Stevens. How may I help you?" The same voice, unmistakable.

"Mom!"

The silence lasted so long that she thought she'd been cut off. Finally a breathless voice. "Andrea, is that really you?"

"Yes, truly."

"It's been so long . . ."

"I know. Can I see you? Soon? Now? Oh, Mom . . ."

"Let's see. Yes, of course. Hold on a minute . . . Let me think. I usually work till about six, but I can take a tea break now. I'm in the Phipson building downtown. D'you know it? There's a little restaurant on the main floor. Take a cab. I'll pay if you're short."

Andrea pulled out her remaining change and scanned it quickly. "I'll be okay. I'm on my way. Love you."

"Love you times twenty."

Fifteen minutes later she was standing outside the Phipson Tower, and there was Mom sitting at a table in the small restaurant on the street. *Why, she hasn't changed a bit,* was Andrea's first thought. But after they hugged and sat down and stared at each other, she began to realize that this *was* a different Mom. She was sure of herself. She even looked taller, and her clothes were neat, plain but perfect. She wondered if Mom, like Crystal, had her secret sources of inexpensive clothes that looked great.

Meanwhile her mother was staring at her. "You look wonderful, darling. I'm so glad you've had your hair cut. And your clothes are even nicer than those I used to get you. I was afraid that your father might be too strict—he had some funny ideas on how to raise daughters."

Andrea smiled. She wasn't about to tell Mom that Father hadn't yet seen the new Andrea and would probably have a fit when he did.

Mom poured tea. "Seeing you again is like a miracle. Obviously he's relented. When did he give you my phone number? Will he let you spend weekends with me? I asked so often, but he never would . . ."

"So you did write to *me*? Not just to Father?"

"Of course I did. Darling, I don't mean to reproach you, but why didn't you answer any of them?"

"Oh!" Andrea put down the sandwich she had just picked up. "I never saw them."

"You mean you never got them? Not one?"

Andrea shook her head. She saw anger flash in her mother's eyes. Then Mom said, "No. I promised myself that I wouldn't be angry. I'm sure he thought in his odd way that he was doing it for the best—that I was a bad influence on you. But, oh love, that's not important! What matters is—have you been happy? And is everything all right in school? It's such a big step, going into high school, isn't it? So many changes and so much extra work, but I'm sure your father helps."

"He's pretty busy." Andrea evaded a direct answer. "He doesn't say much."

Her mother sighed and rubbed her hands over her face. "Maybe I should have kept you, but I'd no money and I was pretty rocky, on the verge of a nervous breakdown. It seemed for the best that you should stay where you'd be secure."

"It's okay," Andrea said quickly and put her hands over her mother's. "I'm beginning to understand him a little. And I've changed." She hesitated. It would be wonderful to share with Mom the feelings, the memories—or were they dreams?—the sense of somehow having grown into her body, of becoming the person she was supposed to be. But she realized that even Mom wouldn't believe it. And the more she thought about it, the mistier her memories became, until she could hardly believe it herself. "I've changed," she repeated. "School was tough at first, but I think it's going to be all right now that I've got a handle on it and I'm starting to take charge of my own life."

"Darling, I'm *so* proud of you. You have no idea." Mom reached across the table to squeeze Andrea's hand. "Taking charge of your own life. That's the most important thing of all. My dear, you are growing up so beautifully." She looked at her watch. "And now I have to fly. We must stay in touch, love. You might not know—I don't know how much your father has shared with you—but I made him a promise that I wouldn't—"

"I know," Andrea interrupted. "I read your letters to him. I know I shouldn't have, but I'm glad I did. I had to find out what was going on. And I'm fifteen and old enough to make up my own mind. As soon as I get home I'll tell him we've met and we're going to keep on meeting. I don't suppose . . . ?" She hesitated.

"I've got a small apartment, all my own, and there's a tiny spare room to which you're welcome on weekends, if you can square it with your father. Though if there is a problem . . ." She chuckled.

"When I left I had no money at all and no job possibilities, or so it seemed to me. Now I've learned I was wrong. I've got plenty of smarts and my education wasn't as feeble as your father made out. So now I work for a couple of lawyers who, I'm sure, would back me up if there's ever a fight over shared custody."

"It won't come to that," Andrea said confidently. "We'll work it out. Love you."

"Love you times twenty." They kissed and Andrea watched her mother pay the bill and walk quickly out of the restaurant. She sat back with a sigh and began to eat from the tier of tiny sandwiches and cakes. *I'm starving*, she realized. When she finished, she licked her fingers, picked up her backpack, and strolled out into the sunshine. Life was absolutely perfect. But she still had one piece of unfinished business.

Wasn't Sofia's store somewhere in this neighbourhood? She had the sudden impulse to visit it right now, and she set off down the street until she came upon the alley in which it was hidden. OPEN, the sign said, and she opened the door and went in. The chime above the door tinkled. The owl stared at her solemnly. The grandfather clock's two hands still pointed at twelve. *Nothing's changed since I ran away from the Six and found refuge in this cosy place. And why should anything have changed?* she thought. *It's only been a day.*

Then she frowned. *But it wasn't yesterday, was it?* She slipped off her backpack and drew the small black oblong from the side pocket. She ran her fingers over the silver inlay. *Not just a design*, she remembered. *A maze.*

The maze grew warm, and memories tumbled through her head as she held the box. Scissors and fire. A swampy Cretaceous world. Guns and the war. More guns and the Wild West. A desert and, in the end, an oasis she made for her old enemy.

*I can do that again*, she thought with a sudden rush of happiness. *Make an oasis in my heart when things get tough. Peace, like Sabrina's peace. If I can only remember how.*

She was still smiling, running her thumb absently over the black box, when the curtain to the back room was pulled aside and Sofia emerged. "No amulets today, I'm afraid."

Andrea laughed. "So you do remember me. I think you were teasing me yesterday." She held out the black box. It lay cool in her hand. "Maybe it's not an amulet. I'm not really sure what it's for, but it seems to have brought me luck—all the luck I need. So I thought I'd return it to you. And maybe buy a couple of gifts." She dug in her jeans pocket. "I don't have too much money left, but maybe enough, if you'll advise me."

"What are you looking for?"

"A kind of keepsake for a new friend, a girl my

own age. And for my father . . ." She hesitated. "That's a great deal more difficult. Perhaps a book? He reads a great deal of mathematics and philosophy and stuff like that." She looked hopefully at the crowded bookshelves.

Sofia waved her hand at the box of oddments through which Andrea had sifted in her search for an amulet. Without meaning to, her hands closed over a pendant with a stone that reminded her of something—what could it be? It was a blue stone with flecks of white in it. She held it up. "This is exactly right."

Sofia nodded. "An excellent choice. It brings with it the promise of healing and new beginnings."

Andrea put it down on the counter and began to browse through the collection of dusty leather-bound books that crammed the shelves of the bookcase. One seemed almost to fall into her hand and she opened it curiously. Inside the front cover was an autograph in spidery ink. It looked old and interesting.

"Yes, of course," Sofia said softly. "I should have thought of that myself. Your father is perhaps a somewhat austere and private person?"

"Why, yes."

"The perfect choice." Sofia placed the pendant with its blue stone in a tiny box, covered it with a twist of rainbow-coloured paper, and then wrapped the book in a silk handkerchief, itself as good as a gift, and tied with a piece of gold cord. "You are sure you don't want to keep the maze?"

Andrea shook her head. "I don't seem to have a use for it. You see, my whole life has changed and I guess I don't need it any more. Thank you for the thought." She looked at the black box with the delicate design traced in silver upon its top and found herself wondering what it could really have been for. *A maze*, Sofia had called it. What a curious name.

But that didn't matter right now. It was time to go home and face the music. To tell Father that she'd spent almost the whole of the hundred and fifty dollars on herself and that she had found and met her mother and, moreover, fully intended to go on meeting her.

*Outrageous! He'll kill me!* Her courage almost failed her, and she reminded herself that she had stood up to him before and she could do it again. She pushed the front door open. He was waiting for her.

"You are very late, Andrea. What have you been—" he began and then stopped in mid-sentence to take in her transformed appearance. He didn't look angry, the way she expected. Instead he drew back and his face was suddenly white with shock.

"Wh–what's the matter, Father?" she stammered. "Are you ill?"

"You look just like—you remind me of your mother when I first met her. It's extraordinary—unsettling."

"I look the way she did? I didn't know that, but I'm glad. I had my hair cut." She touched her hair. "It was long overdue, Father. And I spent the rest of the money you gave me on clothes that were more suitable, that don't make me a laughingstock at school," she added in a rush of words.

He said nothing, but continued to stare at her. He took off his glasses to rub his eyes and without them he looked suddenly vulnerable. Now she felt shy rather than scared, as if he were someone she had only just met. She hurried to fill up the awkward silence with words.

"I almost forgot. I went into a funny little antique store and I found this. I thought you might like it." She handed him the silk-wrapped book. "If you hate it, I can easily take it back," she added quickly, as he undid the cord and folded back the silk handkerchief.

He stared at it and then at Andrea. "Alfred North Whitehead. *Science and the Modern World.*" He opened it "1925! A first edition. And autographed. That is truly amazing!" He stepped toward her, as if to give her a hug, then settled for a pat on her arm and another distracted "thank you." He was about to wander off into his study, book in hand, when she stopped him.

"Two more things, Father. I hope you're not going to be too shocked or angry or anything, but I've met Mom. We had tea."

"I might have guessed. I presume she was responsible for your hair and clothes?"

"No. Actually I did that all by myself. I didn't want to meet her looking the way I did. I thought she might be shocked. I didn't want her blaming you for my appearance," she added craftily.

"Blaming *me*?" He stared at her, his face bewildered.

"Anyway, I really want to spend alternate weekends with her if that's okay. She has a little apartment with a spare room."

"Weekends? But how am I to manage? That's when we buy groceries. That's when you houseclean and do the laundry."

Andrea felt a small stab of pain. He didn't want *her* company on the weekends, only *his* comfort and convenience. She told herself not to be angry. Not everything in the world had changed, just because she and Crystal and Sabrina had. For Father to change was going to take a very long time. *But I'll work at it*, she promised.

"Groceries and housekeeping. That can be fixed," she said gently. "I know you can afford some help— a housekeeper maybe. Pretty soon I'll be too busy with schoolwork to do as much in the house anyway. Maybe *you* could learn to cook yourself," she added outrageously, at which he turned into his study with a grunt. But he was still cradling her gift lovingly in his hands.

Andrea let out her breath and ran her fingers through her unfamiliar hair. She'd done it! He hadn't exploded and the world hadn't come to an end. Tomorrow she would give the pendant with its strangely familiar stone to Crystal as a thank-you gift for helping her with the new clothes and hairstyle. It would be the promise of healing and new beginnings. *The stone*, she thought again, and a sudden flash of memory echoed in her ears. "The stone at the heart of the maze," Sofia had said. *Maybe it'll be as lucky for her as that black box seems to have been for me*, she thought.

"We're fresh out of amulets," Sofia had said.

Maybe not.